ADVENTURES of a CAT-WHISKERED GIRL

ADVENTURES of a CAT-WHISKERED GIRL

BY
DANIEL PINKWATER

ILLUSTRATIONS BY
CALEF BROWN

HOUGHTON MIFFLIN BOOKS FOR CHILDREN
Houghton Mifflin Harcourt
Boston New York 2010

Jennifer Laughran
—*Bonus procurator est rarus quam
bonus scriptor.*

Houghton Mifflin Books for Children is an imprint of
Houghton Mifflin Harcourt Publishing Company.

www.hmhbooks.com

The text of this book is set in Apollo MT.
The illustrations were created in brush and ink.

Library of Congress Cataloging-in-Publication Data

Pinkwater, Daniel Manus, 1941–
Adventures of a cat-whiskered girl / by Daniel Pinkwater.
p. cm.
Summary: Big Audrey, who has cat-like whiskers, and her telepathic friend, Molly,
set out on a journey to find out why flying saucers are landing behind the old stone
barn in Poughkeepsie, New York, and, more importantly, to determine whether
another cat-whiskered girl really exists.
ISBN 978-0-547-22324-7
[1. Extraterrestrial beings—Fiction. 2. Cats—Fiction. 3. Science fiction. 4. Humorous
stories.] I. Title.
PZ7.P6335Ad 2010
[Fic]—dc22
2009049704

Manufactured in the United States of America
DOC 10 9 8 7 6 5 4 3 2 1
4500221577

CONTENTS

i. Explaining

It surprises me how many people don't know there are different planes of existence. Well, it's not really surprising that you don't know if no one ever explained it to you, so I will do that now. Imagine that you live in a house that is all on one level: no upstairs, no downstairs, no attic, no basement, no crawlspace underneath. You live there, and you go in and out, and everything seems normal. Now imagine that it is really a three-story house, and you live on the second floor, with people living above you and below you . . . but you never know it! You never see the people living above and below, you never hear them, you don't know anything about them—and they don't know anything about you. There are three families living in the same place, at the same time, and each family thinks they are the only one.

It's like that, only it's not houses, it's whole worlds. And there is one other thing to imagine. Imagine the three floors of the imaginary house all squashed together, so it's only one story again, but the people *still* have no idea they are not alone. This part is tricky to imagine. Let's say you are in your bedroom, listening to music, lying on your bed, and bouncing a rubber ball off the ceiling. At the same time, in the same space as your bedroom, someone you can't see or hear is giving the dog a bath, and someone else you can't see or hear (and the dog-bather can't see or hear) is preparing vegetable soup.

It gets more complicated. While you are bouncing a ball off the ceiling, and someone else is bathing the dog, and someone else is making soup, a highway with traffic is running right through your bedroom, or there is a herd of buffalo wandering around, or there's a river with water and fish in it. All at once, and all at the same time. But if you are in any of the worlds all going on at once, it looks and feels to you like there is only one.

Now imagine this: sometimes it is possible to go from one world to another. It's really rare, but it does happen. There you are bouncing a ball off the ceiling, and next thing you know you are in the middle of a herd of buffalo. Or, if you were to catch a momentary glimpse of someone from another plane of existence, you'd probably mistake them for a ghost. I know about all this—I myself came from another plane of existence to this one.

A skeptical person might think I was making all this up, or that I was crazy if I believed it myself. Of course, anyone can say she comes from another plane, or planet, or that her mother is the queen of Cockadoodle (which is not a real place, as far as I know). Well, it's true that I can't absolutely prove I come from another plane. However, if you go to the library and get ahold of encyclopedias and *National Geographic*s and certain books, you can find an article with pictures of a typical-looking Inuit, a typical-looking Northern European, a typical-looking Mongolian, a typical-looking Bantu, Korean, Australian, Moroccan, and so on . . . all different types. All different in minor ways, and all similar in most ways. It is interesting. What you will not find is a picture of a girl with cat whiskers and sort of catlike eyes. That is, until they take a picture of me.

II. Where I'm From and Where I Was

Since practically nobody even suspects there are other planes of existence, there would be no reason to name the one you live on. Besides, if the one I came from had a name, nobody on this one would have ever heard of it. I lived in a city, an ordinary city, with my uncle, Uncle Father Palabra. He's a retired monk and a professor of mountain-climbing. I don't remember my parents very well—they went away a long time ago. I liked living with my uncle, and I was reasonably happy, but for some reason I developed a strong desire to travel to other places and see things. I met three kids, Yggdrasil, Neddie, and Seamus, who had managed to get off their plane and onto mine. We got to be friends, and when they went home, I went with them. My name is Big Audrey.

Yggdrasil (or Iggy), Neddie, and Seamus live in a city called Los Angeles. I stayed with them for a long time, and I even got a job in an all-night doughnut shop. Doughnuts are not unknown where I come from, but they are not used as food. I had fun working in the doughnut shop, and got to observe the many varieties of life-forms that came there, especially late at night.

iii. Where I Went

I went to Poughkeepsie, New York. I said goodbye to my friends Iggy and Neddie and Seamus, and also to Crazy Wig. Crazy Wig is a friend of theirs. He is a shaman, which means he can see visions and knows things of a mysterious nature. The first time I met Crazy Wig, he grabbed my head with both hands, closed his eyes, and made odd sorts of singing noises while continuing to hold my head. Then he said, "Daughter, your destiny is not here. You must travel. You must go on a quest. You must go . . . the vision doesn't say where, but you have to go there."

A couple weeks later, Crazy Wig arranged for me to go as a passenger with this movie actor he knew, a guy by the name of Marlon Brando, who was driving his car to New York, which is all the way on the other side of the continent. I had been thinking I should see more of this plane of existence than just Los Angeles anyway, so I quit my job at the Rolling Doughnut, threw my few belongings into a bag, and took off with Marlon in his big convertible.

Marlon was extremely handsome, and crazier than a bat. He talked incessantly about health food and played bongo drums while driving. He drove fast, and we went nonstop. Marlon had plenty of fruit, wheat germ, and bean curd in the trunk (and also a dozen large chocolate cakes, which did not seem like health food to me), so we never stopped at restaurants—just to gas up the car. When he got tired, he'd pull over, eat about half a chocolate cake, wash it down with carrot juice, crawl into the back seat, and sleep for a couple of hours. I'd curl up on the front seat with my coat over me. I made it almost all the way to New York City with him, but about the time we reached

Poughkeepsie, I'd had all I could stand and told him I'd be staying there awhile. Marlon gave me a bottle of papaya juice, wished me the best of luck, and bongoed off in a cloud of dust. He was a nice guy, but he got on my nerves.

CHAPTER 1

The UFO Bookshop

I woke up in my little room behind the shop, washed, got the big electric coffee porcolator started, and got ready to open the shop. This had been my routine since I first hit town. Mr. and Mrs. Gleybner had hired me on the spot when I walked in the door, carrying my bag and my bottle of papaya juice.

"Oh! Look, dear!" Mrs. Gleybner, who was short and round, said.

"Oh! Yes, dear!" Mr. Gleybner, who was also short and round, said.

"You are just the employee we have been wishing for," Mrs. Gleybner said.

"You will like working here," Mr. Gleybner said.

"Do you come from . . . a long way away?" Mrs. Gleybner asked.

"Yes. Los Angeles," I said. "My name is Big Audrey."

Mr. and Mrs. Gleybner looked at each other. "Los Angeles, she says." They smiled and nodded knowingly.

The UFO Bookshop specializes in books about flying saucers, visitors from other planets, space travel, aliens who live among us, radio messages from space, and secret government conspiracies to conceal the truth from the people. They also have books about the abominable snowman, Bigfoot, crop circles, the Bermuda Triangle, mystery spots where gravity works backwards, secret cities underneath the surface of the earth, and chickens who can foretell the future. They didn't have any books that told about other planes of existence, but except for that it seemed they had plenty of stuff that would appeal to intelligent people.

The store also had a small selection of binoculars, special notebooks with boxes printed on the pages for noting characteristics of flying saucers you'd see, pens that had a little flashlight built in, and cards with pictures of different kinds of spaceships on one side and different kinds of space beings on the other, for quick identification. There was also the Gleybner Helmet, which was something like a colander with wire spirals sticking out of it and a chinstrap—this was to enhance the reception of telepathic brainwaves from the space people. Mr. Gleybner made them in the basement.

Naturally, the Gleybners had assumed I was an extraterrestrial alien because of my appearance. I tried to explain, but their minds were made up. They wanted me to work for them, paid me the same as I had gotten working at the Rolling Doughnut in Los Angeles, and threw in the room in the back for me to live in. I liked the store, and I liked them. Also, once I got started working there, I found out that Mrs. Gleybner brought delicious homemade sweeelves in the morning, and wonderful soup for lunch. Supper time, they would send me to the delicatessen or the Chinese restaurant, and we would eat at the table in the back of the store.

During the day, I would dust and vacuum, unpack books, and wait on customers, and when nothing was happening I could read. Mrs. Gleybner spent a good part of each day visiting with other shopkeepers on the street, and Mr. Gleybner would read, work at his desk, and take naps in his rocking chair. There was a store cat named Little Gray Man, and he and I got to be very good friends.

The best thing about working in the UFO Bookshop was the customers.

"The finest and most interesting people in all Poughkeepsie come into this shop," Mr. Gleybner said.

Of course, I did not know all the people in Poughkeepsie, but the ones who came into our shop were mostly very satisfying to observe and talk with.

CHAPTER 2

Letters

I sent a letter to Yggdrasil telling about things I was learning. I told her how Alexander the Great had seen two flying saucers in 329 B.C., how Edmund Halley, who discovered Halley's Comet, saw one in 1676, how Christopher Columbus had seen one in 1492, and how one was seen in 1783 from Windsor Castle in England. I also told her about Little Gray Man, and how nice the Gleybners were to me.

She wrote back to me that Crazy Wig had seen the word "Poughkeepsie" in a vision and said it had something to do with my destiny, and that everybody there sent their love.

I also wrote to Iggy about Poughkeepsie.

Dear Iggy,

Poughkeepsie is different from Los Angeles. It is an old city, about 300 years old! There are strange-looking old houses, and some of the streets curve and bend and go every which way. There are lots of trees, and a creek twists and turns through the city. In the old days, the creek turned water wheels that powered mills and factories that made piano keys, cough drops, ladies' underwear, buggy whips, licorice whips, and buttonhooks, and some of them are still there. A big river runs past, and there is a ridiculously high and precarious-looking railroad bridge that goes over it. There are trolley cars that run on tracks, and a gigantic madhouse on the north side of town. And even though it's a city it's surrounded by country—you cross a street and all of a sudden it's farms and forests. There are wild bunnies, rats, and opossums in the business district. The people like to eat jitter-bugs, which is the name of a dish consist-ing of a slice of white bread with a slice of meatloaf on it, and on top of that a scoop of mashed potato, all of it covered with brown gravy. I haven't tried one—too disgusting—but they are sold everywhere. I spend all my spare time exploring.

Give my love to Neddie and Seamus, Crazy Wig, and all our friends.

Audrey

CHAPTER 3

People

I missed my friends in Los Angeles, but I wasn't lonely. People came into the bookstore every day, and most of them liked to talk. And it was only a half-block to Main Street, where the bigger stores were, and lots of people. Also, there was a trolley, or streetcar, that ran on tracks from the loony bin, and patients who weren't considered dangerous would come every day to walk around, sit on the benches, and watch the normal people. A lot of the loonies were interesting to talk to. And of course, some people were both mental patients and customers.

I do not have a problem with my appearance—I am a nice-looking girl with lovely whiskers. But some people do tend to stare or ask silly questions. I got a lot less of this in Poughkeepsie than I had in Los Angeles.

The bookstore customers were all sure, like the Gleybners, that I was an outer-space alien girl. I learned to
avoid specifically saying whether I was or was not. It
meant a lot to them, thinking I was. Besides, I sort of
am. The loonies tended not to mention the whiskers.
I think they weren't sure if they were seeing them or
hallucinating.

Probably my favorite customer, and also my favorite loony, was Professor Tag from Vassar, a girls' college not far from Main Street. He was a cute little old
guy with a tangled gray beard. He talked fast and was
always excited about something. If you didn't know
he was a professor, you would have thought he was a
bum. I liked him because he was always smiling and
laughing, and because he liked me.

Once a year, Professor Tag would go nuts and they
would move him up to the loony bin for a while—then
he'd get over being nuts and they'd bring him back to
teach his classes. He told me all this himself, and sure
enough, a little while later he went nuts. I asked the
Gleybners why he hadn't been in the store for a while,
and they told me he was up at the insane asylum for
his annual cure. So one Sunday I took the streetcar up
to the place to visit him.

The insane asylum was big and sad and scary. It
was not just a building as I had imagined. It was a lot

of buildings, like a whole not-so-little town. The main building was the biggest. It looked like a scary castle. The streetcar stopped in front of it, and I went in the main entrance to the office and told them I was there to visit Professor Tag. The lady in the office picked up a phone and talked to someone. Then she told me I could go outside and sit on a bench and Professor Tag would be along.

There was a very large lawn sloping down from the main building, with some benches facing it. The lawn ended in trees, and beyond them I could see the mountains on the other side of the river. There were a few people sitting on some of the benches, and others strolling around, or just standing—patients, I guess, or people who worked there, or visitors like me. I picked a bench and was enjoying the view when I became aware of someone standing behind me.

It was a girl about my age, but short and tiny with biggish hands and feet. She was looking over the top of the bench at the mountains in the distance, but it didn't seem that she was seeing them. I was pretty sure she was blind for a minute or two until she shifted her gaze and looked directly at me with strange blue eyes that seemed to shimmer.

"My ancestral home is over there," she said. I

couldn't tell for sure if she was talking to me or to herself.

"In those mountains?" I asked.

"Yes. I come from there," she said. "Anyway, my family came from there. And you come from another plane of existence."

"I do!" I said. "You are the first person who knew that."

"I notice lots of things other people don't," she said. "I'm intelligent."

"Is that why you're here? Did they make you come to this hospital because you notice things other people don't?"

"No. I'm actually nuts," she said. "They put me here hoping to cure me of it."

"And are they doing you any good?" I asked.

"Not really. I'm hoping it goes away by itself. My name is Molly."

"I'm Big Audrey," I said.

"By the way, I like the whiskers," Molly said.

"Everybody does," I said.

"I notice you're not a patient," she said. "You don't look miserable enough."

"I'm here to visit someone. Do you know Professor Tag?"

"Oh, he is practically my favorite person here," Molly said. "Do you miss your parents very much?"

"I don't even remember my parents. They went away when I was very small. My uncle raised me."

"Yes, but do you miss them a lot?" Molly asked.

Something I had noticed talking to the loonies who come down to Main Street is that very often when crazy people are not actively being crazy, they are less crazy than regular people who are a little bit crazy at all times. When Molly asked me if I missed my parents a lot, I realized that I did miss them—even though I couldn't remember them. I had been missing them all my life. It surprised me that I had never figured this out before, and it hit me kind of hard.

"Yes, I do," I said to Molly. "Thanks for asking."

All kinds of thoughts were running through my brain. I must have noticed it before, but it struck me just at that moment that Uncle Father Palabra had never told me much about my parents. All he ever told me was that they went away when I was very small. I must have asked him questions about them, but I couldn't remember him giving any answers. After a while, I must have just stopped asking. And also, just at that moment, it struck me that feeling I didn't fit in where I was, and wanting to see other places and other planes of existence, probably had something to do with my mother and father not being there. And all this stuff had been tucked away in my head, and I never thought about it until this loony girl had asked me if I missed them—and why did she assume they were not with me and were to be missed? She must have read my mind, my subconscious mind.

"There's a big house not far from here, a mansion actually, and the people who live there swing from trapezes with chimpanzeeses."

At first I thought Molly had simply changed the subject and was telling me something factual, and then I realized that her craziness must have just cut in.

"Um, that's interesting," I said.

"We ought to go there sometime," she said. "It would be interesting to see."

Professor Tag appeared from around the corner of the building. He was wearing a woman's dress, sort of—it looked like he had made it out of a big window curtain. He had made a wig out of what looked like the business end of a mop, and he was singing an old song called "Someone Left a Biscuit on the Landing."

"Ah, Audrey! You came to visit me! And I see you have met Molly, a wonderful girl."

"Hello, Professor," I said. "Yes, I came to see you."

"Thank you," Professor Tag said. "As God is my witness, I'll never be hungry again."

"I didn't realize you'd been hungry," I said.

"It's a line from a movie," the professor said. "Scarlett O'Hara says it in *Gone With the Wind*."

"Does he think he's Scarlett O'Hara? Does he think he's a lady?" I asked Molly.

"It's possible," Molly said. "He thinks he's people."

"Come, ladies. Let us sit on this bench and tell sad stories of the death of kings. And no, I do not think I am Scarlett O'Hara. It's a joke, because Scarlett O'Hara made a dress from window curtains, and my dress is made of window curtains."

"And is there any particular reason you are wearing a dress?" I asked. "Not that it isn't a very nice one."

"Thank you," Professor Tag said. "Allow me to introduce myself, or anyway, the person I think I am. I am Sir Edward Hyde, Third Earl of Clarendon, also known as Viscount Cornbury. I am the governor of this colony, and the town of Hyde Park, just to the north of here, is named after me."

Professor Tag said this in such a high-toned way that I felt the only appropriate thing to do was stand up and curtsy to him. Molly did the same.

"And the dress is because . . . why?" I asked.

"Oh, as Lord Cornbury it was my custom to dress up in women's clothing and go walking in the evening. Also, I liked to hide in the bushes and jump out at passersby and scare the spit out of them."

"This is good," I said to Molly. "Here's a loony imagining himself to be some other loony."

"You should have been here yesterday," Molly said. "He thought he was Lewis and Clark."

CHAPTER 4

Talking Crazy

I hope I am not speaking out of turn," I said to Molly. "But you don't seem nearly as wacky as the professor here."

"Oh, he's about at the top of the tree—at least for patients allowed to walk around loose," Molly said. "We're all proud of him."

"Did you have the blueberry pancakes this morning, Molly dear?" Professor Tag asked. "They were extra scrumptious."

We were strolling around the grounds now, the three of us. Other patients and visitors were strolling too. I have to say, it was a pleasant and restful place, even if the buildings looked like the set for a scary movie and there was a fence with iron bars all around the property.

"I see the shuffleboard court is not in use," Professor Tag said. "If you like, I could check out the equipment and we could have a game."

We declined.

"This place is a little like a resort or a hotel," I said.

"That's the theory of it," Professor Tag said. "It's an old-fashioned idea, but as good as any, I suppose. The place itself is supposed to cure us. They provide pleasant and handsome accommodations . . . that is, pleasant and handsome according to nineteenth-century ideas— that's when all these big insane asylums were built. They provide decent food, nice grounds to walk in, diversions and simple tasks for those who can do them, and people are supposed to get well."

"Does it work? Do people get well?" I asked.

"Some do, but they might have anyway. Incidentally, I don't know how late you were planning to stay, but there is an excellent film this evening, *The Snake Pit*. It's a wonderful comedy. I've seen it several times."

"What about you?" I asked Molly. "I mean, in what way are you crazy? I can see how the professor is—he's just a regular insane person."

"And one of the very best," Molly said.

"Thank you," the professor said.

"Credit where credit is due," Molly said.

"But you're not like him. Why are you on the inside?" I asked.

"Oh, it's because I notice things," Molly said.

"But before you said that wasn't why you're in here."

"I also lie," Molly said. "No, that was a joke. What I mean to say is, in addition to noticing things anyone might notice, I also notice things going on in people's heads."

"Like reading minds?"

"Yes, and I also read trees and rocks and things. I can read places. This place, the hospital, is very sad reading, I can tell you. Not everyone enjoys being crazy like the professor here."

"So, what am I thinking right now?" I asked Molly.

"You're wondering if I wasn't lying when I said that I lie," Molly said. "You're wondering if what I am saying is true and whether you can trust me."

"That's more or less right," I said.

"Is it more or is it less?"

"More."

"And, by the way, you can, if you want to."

"Can what?"

"Trust me."

"So what is the professor thinking?"

"He's thinking about how many cows could be put to graze on the hospital lawn."

"Forty-two!" the professor said. "I would suggest Guernseys. They're very nice cows."

"So they put you in here because you can read minds? Why would they do that if you really can?"

"Well, to begin with, they think I can't. They think I'm imagining it. And then there are the voices."

"Voices?"

"I hear 'em. It's one of the big signs that you're cuckoo."

"Are they real voices or voices because you're cuckoo?"

"They're in my head. They sound real to me, but that is what every voice-hearing loony thinks."

"Whose voices are these, and what are they saying?"

"No idea about who. And they seem to be talking to one another, not to me. It's like . . . well, did you ever pick up the phone and hear another conversation faintly going on in the background?"

"I think so. Are you able to make out what they're saying?"

"Not usually. I have an idea they are not of this world."

"Like ghosts?"

"Maybe ghosts, or little men in flying saucers, or maybe they aren't there at all and I'm a nutcase. It's puzzling."

CHAPTER 5

Walkabout

While we talked we had been walking. Away from the big spooky castle of a main building and the big lawn, there were trees, streets, and houses, bungalows, little apartment houses, playgrounds, a little old-fashioned schoolhouse that appeared to be closed, a church. Some of the houses were for the people who worked at the old insane asylum and their families. It really was like a little town.

"When I was quite a small child, my father, Professor Tag, would take me to New York City of a Sunday."

"Your father was a professor too?"

"No, that was his first name. He worked for a commercial dairy in the town of Poughkeepsie. I am named after him, and I am also a professor, so my name and title is Professor Professor Tag. Anyway, in those days, men would sell things in the street. I remember a wonderful toy. It was a limber dancing man, with stretchy arms and legs made of accordion-pleated crepe paper, with a cardboard head, hands, and feet.

"The sidewalk sellers would make them dance amazingly, and they also—though I did not know or understand it—would conceal in their mouths a tiny device known as a ventrilo, with which they would make music and funny noises. Understand, I was very small, and didn't have any knowledge of mechanical things, and I was nearsighted and not yet fitted for glasses, so I never saw the thin black thread by which the dancing men were suspended, and was unable to figure out that a paper toy would not be able to dance by itself.

"I begged my father to buy me one of the amazing things, and as it only cost a few coins, he obliged me. I rode home with him, on the train to Poughkeepsie, in a state of high excitement. I was going to amaze my mother, my little siblings, and all of my friends with the magical toy.

"Naturally, when unwrapped, it was nothing but a cheap paper doll with a string attached. It did not dance, let alone make amusing noises. Had my father not been completely inept and ignorant of mechanics, he might have explained to me that it was the skill of the sidewalk salesman that made the doll perform, and perhaps together we might have made some kind of attempt to work it. But he was as baffled as I was and thought we had been cheated —that a useless copy of the dancing man had been fobbed off on us. He swore vengeance on the dishonest tradesman, and made me swear too that I would track him down to the ends of the earth and get my father's thirty-five cents back. And indeed, until I was twenty-one years of age, that was the central concern of my life."

"And?"

"That's all. I got over it."

"That's a very touching story, Professor."

"Thank you."

CHAPTER 6

Through the Gate

We had walked all the way to the back side of the grounds. There was an open gate, and a road beyond it.

"We've come to a gate," I said.

"So we have," Molly said.

"I mean, are you allowed to leave the premises?"

"I don't see anyone stopping us," the professor said.

"So, we can just . . . leave?" I asked.

"Unless you're tired," the professor said. "As for me, I feel like walking more."

"Fine by me," I said.

"Let's go this way," Molly said.

"What you were saying before, about the voices and all that . . ."

"Yes?" Molly said. "Feel free to ask questions."

"Well, I do have one. You spotted me as a visitor from another existential plane. That is something that just about never happens. How do you know about such things?"

"Well, it's my belief that things are very different from what they seem. For example, space . . . space may not be an illusion—or it may—but it is very much easier to get around than is commonly supposed. I think it's possible to get from here to there in a snap."

"I came from my plane of existence to Los Angeles on a bus," I said. "It took under two hours."

"Doesn't surprise me," Molly said. "I have also worked out that people are immortal, or comparatively immortal, so at different times one carries on one's life in various forms and in various places."

"The Hindus believe this," the professor said.

"Then I agree with them," Molly said. "And, I believe there is a finite number of persons— this includes the animating principle of whales, bunny rabbits, microbes, and eggplants. So it's interchangeable parts, and everybody gets to play all the roles, given enough time—which may or may not be an illusion, but anyway works quite differently from the way most people think it does. And given enough time, you will meet everybody—at least everybody you're supposed to meet . . . and then . . . meet them again."

"Very sound reasoning," the professor said. "You should come and teach in my college."

"Wouldn't I have to graduate first?" Molly asked.

"Yes. They have all these silly rules," the professor said.

I was having a hard time remembering that I was taking a walk with two officially crazy people. From my limited experience passing between planes of existence, the things they were talking about didn't sound particularly insane—on the other hand, the professor was wearing a dress made out of curtains from some room in the mental hospital and had spent a good part of his life seeking vengeance on some guy who had sold his father a toy that he thought didn't work, and earlier Molly had been telling me about a house where people swing from trapezes with chimpanzeeses.

"What are your views on interstellar travel and alien species?" the professor asked Molly.

"Well, given that there are untold billions of stars in the universe, stars like our sun, any of which might have planets, and some incredibly large number of those might have conditions conducive to life, I'm of the opinion it is a dead cert that we are not alone.

Of course, it's hard to get all this stuff to behave in my head, because of being deranged, you know."

"You should read my book *Are Flying Saucers from New Jersey?*" the professor said.

"Are they?" I asked.

"Well, I thought they might be when I wrote it," the professor said. "But now I think possibly not. But I am certain one of the main points where lots of them come together is the airspace above Poughkeepsie."

"I know I've seen plenty of them," Molly said.

"Oh, they're up there, all right," the professor said. "And the genius of it is, who would think of looking for them here? People all have the idea that if you want to see UFOs you have to go out in the western desert."

"I've never seen any flying saucers," I said.

"That's because you're always in that bookshop," the professor said. "And a flying saucer bookshop at that. But anyone who has lived here for any length of time has seen them. Here! I'll ask this passerby. You there! Yokel! Have you ever seen a flying saucer?"

A guy in overalls was walking along the road. "Who wants to know?" he asked.

"Just a seeker after truth," the professor said. "Now fess up. Have you noticed any lights in the sky?"

"Quite often, especially on Wednesdays," the guy said. "And I've seen them land behind the old stone barn."

"There you are! The voice of the people! Thank you, my good man."

"Escaping from the nut farm, are you?" the stranger asked.

"Just for the afternoon," the professor said. "The old stone barn, you say?"

"Just down the road," the local said. "Have a nice day!"

CHAPTER 7

The Old Stone Barn

The way we were going was down a road with tidy houses, trees, and yards on both sides. Like a lot of streets in Poughkeepsie, it had once been all farmland, and in some places we could see past the houses to cultivated fields. It was easy to see that the old stone barn was built before the houses—it looked hundreds of years old. And it was stone, and it was a barn, and it had a sign on it that read OLD STONE BARN, and another one that read COCA-COLA, and a blackboard on which was written "Apple Fritters."

Sometimes as you go from one place to another, step into a room or out a door, you suddenly get a mental picture of how you might appear to someone seeing you for the first time. As we entered the small lunchroom that took up a corner of the old stone barn, I got a flash of the three of us: a tiny girl with a strange, crazy gaze, a gray-bearded old man in a makeshift dress, and a tall girl with pussycat whiskers. We must have been fairly noteworthy. But there were no customers in the place to take note—just the proprietor.

Behind the counter was a tremendously fat woman with a hairnet and a red face. "Apple fritters?" she asked, looking at Professor Tag.

"Apple fritters!" the professor said.

Then she looked at Molly. "Apple fritters?"

"Um . . ."

"Apple fritters?"

"I have money," I whispered to Molly. "It's my treat."

"Apple fritters?"

"Well, I . . ."

"Apple fritters?!?" the fat, red-faced, hairneted woman shouted.

"Apple fritters!" Molly shouted back.

Then she looked at me. "Apple fritters?" she hollered at the top of her voice.

"Apple fritters!" I screamed.

"Apple fritters!" the woman yelled, and hustled into the kitchen to make them.

We took seats along the counter.

"You know, I bet she sells a lot of apple fritters for a little neighborhood place like this," Professor Tag said.

The woman reappeared and banged a plateful of apple fritters with powdered sugar on top down in front of each of us.

"Coffee?" she yelled.

"COFFEE!" all three of us yelled back as loud as we could.

"COFFEE!" the woman shouted. Then, with a big smile on her red face, she drew three mugs of coffee from a big percolator and banged them down on the counter, one, two, three.

The apple fritters were delicious

The coffee was fragrant and creamy and hot.

"I was conversing with a bumpkin just now," Professor Tag said to the apple fritter woman. "He said he has seen flying saucers in this vicinity."

"They land in the back," the woman said. "My apple fritters have an interplanetary reputation."

"What, the space men come in for fritters?"

"Space men and space women. I thought you three might be some of them at first."

"Ah. Is that why you stuck to one expression— 'apple fritters'?"

"Some of them don't know a lot of English."

Now, it is a fact that even if you have worked out logically that the odds are vastly in favor of life on other planets, even if you have had experience that supports the idea that travel between worlds is not only possible but common, and even if you have actually seen or otherwise had personal experience of spacecraft or flying saucers, when someone else claims to have had an encounter your first thought is to check out whether they are crazy.

"I am Professor Tag," Professor Tag said. "I am interested in flying saucers."

"I am Clarinda Quackenboss," the fritter woman said. "I am interested in making the best apple fritters in the galaxy."

"When do 'they' tend to stop by?"

"Could be anytime. Sometimes they are around all the time, and sometimes I don't see any for months. But usually it's at night, and for some reason usually Wednesdays."

"Could we examine the area where they land?"

"Help yourselves. It's out back," Clarinda Quackenboss said.

CHAPTER 8

Cats and Bats

In order to get to the back we had to go out of the little lunchroom, and back through the main door and through the old stone barn. It was dark and musty, and there was a disgusting smell.

"What is that disgusting smell?" I asked.

"It smells like about a hundred male cats," Molly said.

"And bats. There are lots of bats here," Professor Tag said. "Look! You can see the little sweeties hanging from the rafters, having their daytime sleep."

"Where are the cats?" I asked. "I don't see them, just smell them."

"Maybe the bats ate them," Molly said.

"Bats don't eat cats. Other way around, if anything," the professor said.

We gulped fresh air when we came out the back door of the old stone barn.

"Let's look around," the professor said.

"What are we looking for?"

"I don't know. Some kind of evidence that saucers have landed here."

"And what kind of place is this?"

I had been sort of expecting an old run-down farm, but this was not that. There were wide lawns, and a driveway leading to a big, strange-looking house a long way off. There were huge trees bordering the driveway on both sides. These trees were like nothing I had ever seen. Their trunks were thick and twisted, with smooth gray bark and weird bulges. The branches were skinny and angular, and bent this way and that, and the roots above the ground were fat and bulbous-looking, like old feet with bunions. The leaves were shiny and metallic-looking, and they shimmered and rustled in the breeze. I had the feeling that the trees towering over us were looking down at us. Somehow they looked as though they could pick up their bulbous roots and walk. They were like . . . intelligent trees! And a little scary and maybe evil.

"It's an old estate," Professor Tag said. "And these are the biggest, oldest, weirdest beech trees I have ever seen."

"Beech trees? Is that what they are?"

"Yes, copper beeches, and some other varieties I don't recognize. They have to be way over a hundred years old."

"Professor, do you get the feeling these trees know we're here?"

"They're very old trees," the professor said. "They may have developed some kind of consciousness in all their years. And they may not be the only ones who know we're here."

I didn't understand what the professor meant at first. Then I saw someone approaching us.

It was a tall old lady with gray hair piled up on her head, wearing a dress not unlike Professor Tag's.

"How do you do?" the professor said. "I am Professor Tag, on temporary leave from the college while insane, and these ladies are Audrey and Molly. Clarinda Quackenboss, the apple fritter lady, said it would be all right for us to come back here and have a look around."

The old lady stood very straight, with her hands folded. She had gray eyes and very pale skin. "I am

Alexandra Van Dood," she said. "You are welcome to look. Do you know where you are?"

"I do and I don't," Professor Tag said. "Clearly this is a very old estate, at least two hundred years old. The beech trees are of remarkable age and size. The mansion is of Dutch design, very large and grand— it must be a famous house. But I have lived in this county and city all my life, and I am a scholar, yet I never knew it was here! Madame Van Dood, will you tell me the name of this house?"

"This is Spookhuizen," Alexandra Van Dood said.

"What? This is Spookhuizen?" The professor was excited. "Of course I have heard of it, but I did not know it still existed—or that it ever existed. This is Spookhuizen, the ancient seat of the Van Vliegende and Van Schotel families?"

"Yes, this is the Vliegende-Schotel mansion," the old lady said.

"And is it haunted, as the stories tell?" the professor asked.

"Oh, it is most haunted," Madame Van Dood said. "Most haunted."

We looked down the avenue of tortured-looking trees. The house was big and dark, and the windows were dark. It was covered with cedar shingles that had turned black over the centuries and had a silvery sheen like the leaves of the beeches. The shadows under the porches were the blackest black. It didn't seem to me like a place in which I would want to set foot in broad daylight, and at night you couldn't pay me to go in.

"We will have to come back here sometime at night," the professor said, causing me to remember he was crazy.

"If you will excuse me, I must go now," Alexandra Van Dood said.

And then she was gone! We looked around in all directions but could not see her going away. But here is the funny thing: I thought I saw a big white owl flitting through the beech trees, Molly thought she saw a white horse galloping over the lawn, and the professor thought he saw a white mouse scurrying through the grass.

CHAPTER 9

Back to Abnormal

Let's be getting back to the madhouse," Professor Tag said. "I need to change out of this hot dress and then check myself out."

"You're going to leave the hospital?" Molly asked.

"Yes, I will cut short my stay, pleasant as it has been," the professor said. "I have some research to do in the library."

"About Spookhuizen?" I asked.

"Yes. I want to know who Alexandra Van Dood was."

"*Was?* Don't you mean *is?*"

"I mean *was*. Don't you know a ghost when you talk to one?"

We walked back along the same road to the nut-hatch. As we walked a little way behind the professor, who was hurrying, Molly and I conversed.

"Let me ask you a question. Do you feel at home here?"

"Here? You mean in Poughkeepsie?"

"I mean on our version of Planet Earth. Do you feel at home here?"

"I suppose I do . . . Anyway, I feel as at home as . . ."

"As you did on the other version of the planet, or plane of existence, from which you came?"

"Yes."

"And let me ask you another question. Did you feel at home there, as though you belonged?"

I thought. "No, I guess not. Not ever. Not for a minute."

"Felt alien?"

"Yes."

"Alien there, and alien here?"

"That is not to say I don't like it here . . . and there—and I love my uncle, Father Palabra. Just that I never felt . . ."

"At home?" Molly said. "By the way, did you know many cat-whiskered people in your home world?"

"Well, it's not all that common, but of course people have them."

"Know any personally?"

"I didn't go to a school, or have a whole lot of friends. Uncle Father Palabra educated me at home."

"Ever see anyone on the bus, or in a store downtown—anything like that?"

"No, now that you mention it . . ."

"Interesting."

It was interesting. Had I just assumed cat whiskers were a normal occurrence? Molly had a way of bringing up things that made me wonder why I had never thought about them before.

CHAPTER 10

Back to Normal

Did you have a nice visit with Professor Tag at the laughing academy, dear?" Mrs. Gleybner asked me.

"He's checking himself out," I said.

"So soon? Usually he stays in until the end of the semester," Mrs. Gleybner said.

"He wants to do some research."

"Such a nice man," Mrs. Gleybner said. "We're thinking of ordering chicken chow mein, Chinese string beans, and egg drop soup. Does that sound all right to you?"

I told the Gleybners about visiting Spookhuizen with Molly and Professor Tag. I was sure they would be interested, but for some reason it didn't seem to make much of an impression. I think they were more concerned with things in books, as distinct from things in real life. I thought probably when the professor found stuff out in his research, if he wrote about it, then they'd be all excited. It may be that so many people came into the shop every week, making so many claims that turned out to be empty, that they just tuned out any firsthand mention of UFOs or similar things. It was even possible that they didn't actually believe in flying saucers and didn't know they didn't. They politely listened when I told them we'd heard that flying saucers had been seen landing behind the old stone barn, and then asked questions about Molly, and whether she was a nice girl, and were they helping her get over being insane at the psychiatric place. They said I could invite her to supper sometime.

I thought a lot about Molly and the professor over the next couple of days. I was thinking I would go back to the loony bin the next Sunday and visit Molly—when she turned up in the store!

"Molly! What are you doing here? Did you take the streetcar from the institution?"

"I lit out, Audrey. I couldn't stand it there anymore. They serve shepherd's pie three times a week."

"Ick. Sounds disgusting. What is it?"

"You don't want to know."

"So, does your family know you graduated yourself from crazy college?"

"Get a hint, Audrey. My family is supernatural. They don't know where I am half the time, and I don't know where they are."

"They're supernatural?"

"Mostly."

"Who or what are they?"

"They're little weird people who live deep in the Catskill Mountains, bowling and brewing gin. They're almost never seen, and they dress like the seven dwarves."

"What, Molly? You're one of those Catskill Mountain elves? The ones sometimes said to be the ghostly crew of the *Half Moon*? The ones who played ninepins with Rip Van Winkle? Funny, you don't look elfish."

"Well, the men are pretty ugly, but we females are nice," Molly said.

"So you're not going back to the Catskills?"

"If I did, and if I could find my family, I'd spend my days crushing juniper berries or herding goats or something. They're completely old fashioned."

"So what are you going to do?"

"I thought I'd hang out with you for a while. I could sleep on the floor."

"The Gleybners have already suggested you come to supper. They're nice. I don't imagine they would object. Tell them you're an elf and they'll insist you stay."

"Not an elf exactly. More of a dwerg or a fee—anyway, something along those lines. By the way, this is Wednesday."

"So it is. What about it?"

"Don't you want to hike up to Spookhuizen tonight and see if any flying saucers land?"

"Oh, I hadn't thought about that! Sure. Let me tell Mrs. Gleybner you're staying to supper, and we can start out right after. It's chicken with peanuts and hot peppers tonight."

"Yum!"

CHAPTER 11

Fuzzing Saucers

Supper was just as I thought it would be. The Gleyb ners were crazy about Molly. The only way they could have liked her more would have been if she told them she was an extraterrestrial alien. But being a Catskill Mountain dwerg, which turns out to be Dutch for "leprechaun," was almost as good. The funny thing was, once they got done saying ooh and aah, and how exciting it was that Molly was descended from the little guys in the story about Rip Van Winkle, they treated her like an ordinary kid, one they liked and were interested in—which was nice. I could tell Molly enjoyed being with the Gleybners. I asked if it would be all right if Molly stayed with me for a little while.

"I can sleep on the floor," Molly said.

"No need for that," Mr. Gleybner said. "We have a perfectly nice folding cot in the closet. I'll just wheel it into your room after supper."

"We're going up to Spookhuizen tonight to see if any flying saucers land," I said.

"Don't get abducted. And take sweaters," Mrs. Gleybner said.

Even though Molly was little, with little short legs, she was a fast walker. I had to stretch to keep up with her.

"I wonder if we'll see flying saucers," I said.

"I hope so," Molly said. "I'm also interested in seeing your reaction to them if we do."

"What do you mean?" I asked.

"Oh, just what you think about them," Molly said. "You're an unusual person."

The apple fritter place was closed and dark, but the main door of the old stone barn was open, and we went in. The bats were awake and flitting around; we could hear their wings rustling. We hurried through and emerged in back with a lot of bats flying over our heads. The moon was already up, and it made the beech trees appear a hundred times spookier; also the roof of the old mansion shone silvery in the moonlight. The place was completely silent, and we breathed quietly and didn't even whisper.

I felt a little scared. It was a perfect setting for a ghost, and I was half expecting to see Alexandra Van Dood, but she never appeared. Molly and I stood in the shadow of the eaves of the old stone barn and watched and waited.

We didn't have to wait long. It was a clear night, and every one of the millions and millions of stars shone brightly. A shooting star flitted this way or that every few minutes. And some of the stars seemed to pulsate or throb . . . and there were some that seemed fuzzy, or blurry, bigger than the other stars, and maybe not so bright. Some of these fuzzy stars moved, but they didn't flit or streak like meteors. After a while, I realized they were moving toward us—and they were not stars but fuzzy places in the sky.

Molly poked me. I poked back. The fuzzy lights were definitely closer, bigger, and they were moving slowly and gracefully across the sky.

And closer. And closer. And showing beautiful colors that changed. And closer.

I had sort of expected machines, metal machines, maybe making machine sorts of noises, maybe clanking, maybe whirring, maybe shooting fire like rockets, maybe with electric lights flashing on and off. It wasn't like that. They were quiet, almost silent—but I could hear them, or feel them. And instead of being things made of metal, solid things, they seemed to be . . . Well, I can't say what they seemed to be. Soft: I knew they were soft. And they were warm. And they made me feel . . . content, and happy, and almost a little sleepy in a pleasant way.

Throbbing, vibrating, thrumming, I could feel it in my bones. And the saucers, more like gigantic fuzzballs, were really close. The whole place was lit up bright as day—only it wasn't bright, it was the softest kind of light. I'd say it was pink, but that is just as close as I can come to describing the color—it was no color I had ever seen. I could hardly take my eyes off the saucers, but I made myself glance at Molly. Her mouth was hanging open and her eyes were staring—just like mine. She looked stunned—happy but stunned. By this time I was experiencing the flying saucer fuzzballs as if they were music. And perfume: an amazing scent, it was like nothing I'd ever smelled—the closest I can describe is pineapple with a hint of mint or maybe catnip. It made me dizzy. And there was a taste in my mouth like the best cookies anyone ever ate, or never ate. It was also like taking a bubble bath.

And that was when they were still a couple hundred feet above us.

By the time they were at the level of the treetops, we were so full of bliss, we were probably drooling.

Also giggling. The fuzzballs bounced around, whirling and zigzagging—it was comical somehow. They were putting on a show for us.

I noticed there were lights flickering in the windows of Spookhuizen. The flying fuzzers bowled down the avenue of beech trees, bounced a couple of times, and settled onto the roof of the house. Then they either sank or extinguished, going out like matches. And it was over. They were gone.

"Wow! That was not what I expected," I said to Molly when I got my voice back. "I loved it! I love the saucers!"

"Did they go inside the house?" Molly asked.

"It sort of looked like it," I said. "But I'm not sure."

There was the house, dark and silent and dead-looking in the moonlight again.

"Do you want to wait around in case they come back?" Molly asked.

"I'm not sure I could stand it if they came back," I said. "I might flip my wig—no offense."

"None taken."

We made our way back through the dark barn. The lights were on in the lunchroom, and we could see the enormously fat Clarinda Quackenboss through the windows, bustling around. We went in. The place was empty except for a couple of orange cats before which Clarinda was in the act of placing saucers.

"Ah, it's those girls!" Clarinda said. "You want apple fritters?"

"We just noticed your lights on," I said. "That was quite a show the saucers put on out back."

"Was it? I didn't notice. Too busy getting things ready," Clarinda Quackenboss said. "I open up on Wednesday nights in case the extraterrestrial aliens want fritters."

"Have any come in so far?" Molly asked.

"I was hoping for a big crowd, but all that's come in tonight are these two." She jerked her thumb at the cats. "You want some more milk with apple fritters crumbled in, kitties? No?"

The cats strolled out through the open door.

"How about you, girls?" Clarinda asked. "Apple fritters?"

"We filled up on Chinese food," I said. "Thanks anyway."

CHAPTER 12

Pussycats

So, you don't bother to watch the saucers on Wednesday nights?" I asked Clarinda.

"I'm too busy. Some nights they come crowding in, demanding apple fritters. Some nights they don't. I don't know why. By the way, they pay in pure gold, and they're good tippers, those space aliens."

"Are they nice? Are they fierce?"

"Oh, they're nice. They're regular pussycats."

"What goes into apple fritters?" Molly asked me as we walked home.

"Apples, of course, and some flour and water, sugar, oil to fry them in, maybe eggs if you use them to make the batter."

"So mostly stuff that isn't very expensive and keeps fairly well?"

"I guess."

"And the space creatures pay in gold, and tip handsomely."

"So she said."

"So, she ought to be able to make a tidy profit running that lunchroom specializing in fritters."

"So?"

"But so far we haven't seen anybody there. Where are all the customers?"

"I don't know. Maybe it gets busy at lunchtime."

"Listen, are you going to tell the Gleybners what we saw?" Molly asked.

"Sure. They're interested in flying saucers, anyway in theory. Why do you ask?"

"Well, if you tell them, they will repeat it to everyone who comes into the store, and that's all the flying saucer fans in Poughkeepsie. Then, next Wednesday there might be a whole crowd of people with binoculars and cameras hanging around Spookhuizen. Who knows? It might scare them away, and we might want to go back for another look. You might have questions you want answered."

"I might?"

"You might."

"Well, that guy the professor talked to the other day knew all about them, and that they landed behind the old stone barn on Wednesday nights. So apparently it's not some secret we discovered."

"Right. It's common knowledge, so we are not witholding anything people couldn't find out for themselves if we don't go into detail with the Gleybners. We can just say we saw lights in the sky—it's the truth, and it's also what everybody says when they see, or think they see, flying saucers."

"I wouldn't want to trick the Gleybners," I said.

"It's not tricking; it's just revealing stuff a bit at a time. I think we should talk to the professor before we let the information spread around too much. Do this for me—I'm insane and you don't want to upset me."

"Well, all right," I said. "I don't see that it makes a big difference one way or the other."

CHAPTER 13

What the Professor Found Out

I haven't been able to find out a thing!" the professor said.

Molly and I were in the living room of his house, a nice little house near the college. The professor was wearing a wizard robe and one of those pointy wizard hats with stars and moons on it. When we asked him, it turned out it didn't have any special significance— he just wore the robe around the house because it was comfortable, and the hat came with it and kept his head warm.

"Not a thing?"

"Well, nothing I didn't know already—there is mention of Spookhuizen here and there, but no records, nothing about exactly where it was built, or that it still stands. And the same with Alexandra Van Dood. There was such a person, but I found nothing about her as a ghost. I've been all through three libraries, looked through newspaper records, phoned librarians in New York City and Washington, D.C., and haven't found a scrap."

"Well, we found out something," I said.

"You did?"

We told the professor all about our visit to Spookhuizen, and the beautiful, fuzzy, made-you-feel-wonderful, flying . . . somethings, and how they may have gone into the house.

"Now you see the limitations of professors like me," the professor said. "I looked in books, and you girls went and looked at an actual something. Well done! Very well done!"

"What now?" I asked.

"Well, it's interesting, isn't it?" Professor Tag said. "I suppose I could write a small article about it, but maybe not. People look askance at those who are interested in flying saucers. It's the sort of thing that would emphasize that I'm crazy, which I am—but why do things that call more attention to it?"

"But I want to know more about those flying things we saw," I said. "It's very important to me."

"It is? Why?"

"I don't know. I just know I felt something when we were watching them. I can't describe it, but it was important."

Molly was smiling.

"In that case, now we know what has to be done!" Professor Tag said.

"We do?"

"Of course we do!"

"What? What has to be done?"

"Isn't it obvious?"

"Um, not quite. Tell us."

"We have to get a look inside the house."

"Inside Spookhuizen?"

"Where else?"

"But it's spooky and scary."

"We'll go in the daytime. It's not as scary then, is it?"

"Maybe not *as*."

"If you need to know, you need to know. Did you feel that the things you saw were scary?"

"Just the opposite. But the house is."

"Things are scary until you know what they are. I'll just go and change clothes."

"Wait! We're going now?"

"Why not? No time like the present. Besides,

aren't you a little hungry? I'll treat you both to apple fritters and coffee."

Professor Tag ran into his bedroom and emerged after a few minutes wearing short pants, boots, knee socks, a jacket with a lot of pockets, and a pith helmet. It was one of those African explorer outfits.

"Who are you supposed to be this time?" I asked.

"Professor Tag!" Professor Tag said. "This is my usual costume for field work and expeditions. See? I have pockets for notebooks, lots of pencils, a tape measure, a compass, a waterproof pocket for my lunch."

"What exactly are you a professor of, Professor?" I asked.

"Classical accountancy. I specialize in dynastic Egyptian bookkeeping."

"And you go on field trips and expeditions requiring all that gear?"

The professor was putting his arms through the straps of a rucksack. "You'd be surprised," he said. "A classical accountant must be ready for every kind of emergency."

The first emergency, or what I thought was an emergency, happened when we arrived at the old stone barn. We went through as usual—there were the scary-looking beech trees, making a long corridor, and at the end . . . no house!

"Where is it?" I asked.

"Where is what?" the professor asked.

"The house!"

"What do you mean?" Molly asked.

"I mean it isn't there! There is no house where the house was!"

"What are you talking about? There is the house, just where it always was."

"No it isn't! Yes it is!" The house was there, just like before. "But just now there was no house there!" I said.

"I didn't see no house," the professor said. "And I do not mean that in an ungrammatical way."

"I didn't not neither," Molly said. "And I do."

"Well, that is strange," I said. "It wasn't and now it is."

"A trick of the light, no doubt," the professor said. "Now let's go have a look at it."

"We're going to go inside?" I asked.

"At least we'll have a peek through the windows," the professor said. "Let's approach."

We began walking along the beech-lined driveway toward the house. It was quite a long driveway. And it turned out to be even longer than it first appeared. We walked and walked, and the house didn't seem any nearer.

We walked some more.

And some more after that.

"You know, we don't seem to be getting any nearer," I said.

"We're not," Molly said. "How can that be?"

"Another trick of the light, perhaps," the professor said. "It may be like a Japanese garden: the landscape is cleverly laid out so the spaces seem large and the distances greater than they are. Only in this case, it's done so a great distance seems small. If the trees near the house were larger than the trees at the far end of the drive, for example, it might make them seem closer."

"So you're saying the house is farther than it seems, and someone made it so the distance would seem less? Why would anyone do that?" I asked.

"Why does anyone do anything?" the professor asked. "Let's walk faster and see if we seem to be making any progress."

We walked faster. We walked faster yet. We trotted. We ran. When we looked behind us, there was a long line of trees. When we looked forward, the house appeared to be just as far away as when we first started.

"It's no use," Molly said. "We can't get near the place."

"It has to be moving away from us as we approach," I said. "Did you ever hear of such a thing?"

"And don't forget, when we first came here you didn't see it at all, and a moment later, when Molly and I looked, it was there and we all saw it. I am thinking you looked first, Audrey, and it hadn't arrived yet. And a moment later, it had!" The professor was making a note in his notebook.

"Okay, I have an idea," I said. "What do you think would happen if we found out the boundaries of the property, left it completely, found our way around to the other side, and approached the house from that direction? What do you think would happen then?"

Molly and the professor looked at me. "We could try it, if we wanted to be thorough and scientific," the professor said. "But I think we all know what would happen."

"The same thing," I said.

"I agree," Molly said.

"So what are we going to do?" I asked. "Give up on getting close to the house?"

"Well, now that we know it doesn't want us to get close, I want to all the more," the professor said. "Oh, look! It's gone!"

We looked. There was no house to be seen.

"I told you it went invisible," I said.

"So you did," Molly said. "Wait! I think it's coming back!"

We could see the house, but dimly, and it was sort of transparent.

"Well, this is beyond me," the professor said. "We need to talk to someone who knows about things like this."

"Do you know such a person?" Molly asked.

"I do, and we are going to see her."

"See who?

"Chicken Nancy, of course," the professor said.

CHAPTER 14

Who? Where?

Who is Chicken Nancy?"

"She knows things no one else does," Professor Tag said. "She's very, very, very old. She's the one to ask about things like invisible, evasive houses."

"And this is someone you know?" I asked.

"I know about her."

"But you've never met her."

"No."

"Well, let's go talk to her," Molly said. "Do you know where she lives?"

"Somewhere around here," the professor said. "She's a local wise woman."

"Somewhere around here meaning this neighborhood, or the city of Poughkeepsie, or this general area?"

"This general area. Somewhere in this county, or maybe the next one."

"So how do you propose to find her? The yellow pages?"

"I rather doubt she'd be listed, or even have a phone. We'll ask around. Someone is sure to know where to find her."

I liked the professor so much, and he seemed to know so many things, and was so confident, that I had to keep reminding myself that he was a five-star maniac. I reminded myself.

"I've worked up an appetite chasing that house," he said. "Who'd like apple fritters and coffee?"

"Good idea," Molly said.

"Good idea," I said. "Something real that we can get our hands on."

"It's the girls! And the professor!" Clarinda Quackenboss said brightly. Then she bellowed, "Apple fritters?"

"But of course," the professor said. "And keep them coming."

"Clarinda," I asked. "Did you know that if you try to approach the old house out back, it moves away from you?"

"There's an old house out back? I never noticed."

"What? You've never seen it?"

"I've never looked. I am interested in apple fritters, and serving my customers. That's the way to run a successful business."

When Clarinda went into the kitchen to make our apple fritters I whispered to the professor, "She isn't a ghost, is she?"

"No, not a ghost. I'm not sure what she is, but she may not be an ordinary human. I suspect you will never see her anywhere but in this fritter shop. Very perceptive of you to notice."

"I'm going to ask her if she knows where Chicken Nancy lives," Molly whispered.

"Why bother?" I whispered back. "She'll just tell you all she pays attention to are apple fritters."

"It will do no harm," Molly said. Clarinda came out of the kitchen with fritters. "Clarinda, do you know where Chicken Nancy lives?"

"You go down the road about a quarter of a mile, and go right at the corner. Then go along that road for almost a mile. You'll see a Christmas tree farm on the right, and a long driveway. Go all the way along the driveway, past the Christmas tree farm. There's an orchard on the left—just keep going until the driveway turns into a footpath through the woods.

Continue on that until you come to a little house, and that's it."

"How come you know that?" I asked.

"I buy apples from the orchard."

CHAPTER 15

She's Very, Very, Very Old

There is the city of Poughkeepsie, and surrounding it is the town of Poughkeepsie, which is bigger and more rural. Still, it is possible to look out certain apartment windows or schoolroom windows in the city of Poughkeepsie and see cows, or fields under cultivation. A Christmas tree farm, and an orchard, and woods are within the city—and there are streetcar tracks that go right out into the country, so a farmer can walk a little way from his house, step onto a trolley, and go into the city and see a movie, or buy something in a store, or go to the dentist. And a city person who lives in a building with an elevator can get out where there are things growing, and forests, and visit the loony bin or maybe see bunnies or deer. It's a very good way to have a city, though I'm sure in time all the fields and pastures will be paved over or built on and it won't be as nice.

We followed the road Clarinda had told us about and found the Christmas tree farm and the driveway. It smelled nice with the fir trees on one side and the apple trees on the other. Then the driveway narrowed into a little path that we followed into the woods. We had to walk single-file until we came to a clearing. The sun was shining down through the trees on a little cottage with a pointy roof. There was a neat vegetable garden beside the cottage, and flowers in pots on the little porch. Also on the porch, sitting on a straight chair, was an old lady. Her skin was brown, her hair was white, and her eyes were very clear and bright. She was wearing a gray old-fashioned-looking dress.

There was a dog, gray and shaggy, lying beside the old lady. As we approached, the dog stood up and we saw that he was very big and very tall. He stood with his head down and looked at us with yellow-brown eyes. The eyes were kind and intelligent. But I could tell this dog was not one to mess with. Anyone who found his way to this little house with bad intentions would soon wish he had never come.

"But you have nothing to worry about, girl from far away," the old lady said. "I will speak to the dog. Weer, this cat-whiskered girl and the two crazy people, one a lot crazier than the other, are just looking for information. They mean us no harm." Weer sank down beside the old lady's chair, but kept an eye on us. "By the way, I know you didn't come seeking it, but I can cure you of being insane while you're here—if you wish."

"I am Professor Tag," Professor Tag said.

"I know all about you," the old lady said. "You go cuckoo every spring, and your students love you."

"You are Chicken Nancy, I presume?" the professor said.

The old lady nodded.

"This is Molly," the professor said.

"You are welcome, Molly," Chicken Nancy said. Her voice was clear and nice to listen to. She had a slight accent, which the professor later told me was Dutch. "You are a fairly long way from the mountains where your ancient dwergish people live. I will make you a cup of tea and remove the slight confusion from your head. Would you like that?"

Molly said she would like it very much.

"And this is Audrey," the professor said.

"Audrey. It's been nearly a hundred years since I saw anyone like you. Come into the house, all of you, and we will have a nice visit."

The inside of the house was even tidier and neater than the outside. The floor was made of brick, the walls were whitewashed, the furniture was wooden, simple and primitive, there were bunches of dried herbs and flowers hanging from the rafters, and there was an iron kettle hanging from a hook in a little stone fireplace and making steam.

Chicken Nancy was quite tall when she stood up. "The kettle is just boiling. I will make tea for all of us, and special tea for this crazy girl. You, Professor, prefer to remain crazy, I believe."

"Yes, I am quite accustomed to it," the professor said. "And I was not as happy when I was sane."

"I understand," Chicken Nancy said. "I was crazy myself for twenty-five or thirty years. It can be pleasant if you have the right kind."

"I have the wrong kind," Molly said.

"Hush. It will be taken care of," Chicken Nancy said. "Now, you came to ask me about something. Please sit at my table, and I will help you if I can."

"We wanted to know about the Vliegende-Schotel mansion," I said.

"I know everything about it. What did you want to know?"

"Everything."

"Fine. I will tell you everything. First, its right name is not the Vliegende-Schotel mansion."

"It's not?" the professor asked. "I thought it was so named because the Vliegende and Schotel families lived there."

"There were no such families," Chicken Nancy said. "The family that built the house was called Van Vreemdeling."

"Van Vreemdeling?"

"Van Vreemdeling. *Vliegende* and *schotel* are Dutch words meaning 'flying saucer.'"

"What? There were flying saucers back then?" I asked.

"Why not?" Chicken Nancy asked. "I am going to guess you have seen them landing behind the old stone barn."

"Yes, we have," Molly said.

"Well, they have been doing that for much longer than I have been alive, and I have been alive a hundred and fourteen years."

"You're a hundred and fourteen years old?"

"Approximately. Records weren't kept very carefully for black people."

"It's remarkable," Professor Tag said. "You don't look a day over ninety. To what do you attribute your youthfulness and vigor?"

"I come from a long-lived family, and I never touch fried food," Chicken Nancy said.

"You were saying, the family was called Van Vreemdeling. And you know this because . . . ?"

"Because I was born on the property—the house was Schiksal-Nanie, which is the proper way of saying my name. It means 'dirge of fate,' or 'elegy of destiny.' And my mother was born on the property. She was owned by the Van Vreemdelings."

"'Owned'? How do you mean 'owned'?" I asked.

"She was a slave. My mother was a slave, and I am the child of a slave."

"How is that possible?" Molly asked. "This is New York. Slavery was in the Southern states."

"Slavery was in the Southern states until the end of the Civil War in 1865," Chicken Nancy said. "There was slavery in New York until about 1827, and even after that fugitive slaves from the South could be pursued and caught here—legally—and sent back south."

"So you were born when your mother was only ten or fifteen years out of slavery," Professor Tag said.

"Yes, and of course she remembered it quite well, and told me all about it. It feels odd to think how recent and how close to home it was, doesn't it?"

"It does indeed," the professor said.

"Sojourner Truth, who was born just across the

river, as a slave, lived until 1883, by which time the electric light and the telephone had been invented and were coming into general use, and she probably saw an early automobile or even took a ride in one."

"Who was Sojourner Truth?" I asked.

"Oh, you had better read up on her," Chicken Nancy said. "She was one of the smartest women of her century, and did important things. I met her more than once. And she began as a slave like my mother. But you want to know about the house and the Van Vreemdelings, and what happened there.

"Cornelius Van Vreemdeling had a brassworks, the first one in the colonies. They spun and stamped things out of brass, especially the popular Van Vreemdeling kwispedor."

"What was that?"

"A cuspidor, a spittoon, thing you spit in—they had them everywhere in those days, and Van Vreemdeling got rich selling them, and bought the big piece of land, and built the big house, and became a member of the aristocracy. He was a patroon spittoon tycoon, and later made another fortune importing pineapples.

"But the Van Vreemdelings were strange, and kept to themselves. The people were uneasy about them, and told strange stories about the things that went on at Spookhuizen."

"The lights in the sky?" I asked.

"Yes, those. And the family had an unusual appearance. I have a portrait of Elizabeth Van Vreemdeling, who was Cornelius's granddaughter and was a friend of my mother's."

Chicken Nancy went to an old bureau, opened a drawer, and took out a very small painting in a frame. She handed it to me. It was a portrait of a girl about my age, wearing old-fashioned clothes.

She had cat whiskers just like mine!

CHAPTER 16

Tea for Three

I was surprised, amazed, and curious. While I was being all those things, and thinking of what I wanted to ask first, Chicken Nancy said, "The water is boiling. I will make the tea. This pot is for all of us, Audrey and Professor Tag—and this little pot is for Molly. This will make you sane."

"What's in it?" Molly asked.

"Mint leaves. I grow them myself."

"And what is in the other tea?"

"Mint also, but yours is a special kind. Take a sip."

"Mint leaves will cure madness?" Molly asked.

"How does it taste?"

"It's good."

"Drink it all up."

"How do you know this will work?" Molly asked.

"I am a one-hundred-and-fourteen-year-old wise woman," Chicken Nancy said. "If I didn't know about things like this, who would?"

"How long until I'm sane?" Molly asked.

"Have you finished your tea?"

"Yes."

"It will have worked by now."

"I feel about the same."

"You weren't all that crazy."

"So I'm cured?"

"Yes."

"Imagine that," Molly said.

"Um, this other tea . . ." Professor Tag began.

"It won't do a thing. Enjoy it. You'll be as crazy as ever," Chicken Nancy said.

"Thank you," Professor Tag said. "It's just that I wouldn't want to do anything to upset the delicate balance of my mind."

"I understand completely," Chicken Nancy said.

Weer had placed his great shaggy head on Molly's knee, and she was scratching him behind the ears.

"Would you like to stay here with Weer and me while you get used to no longer being a nutbar?" Chicken Nancy asked Molly.

"Well, if I am no longer insane, there is no point

going back to the mental hospital," Molly said. "And I don't know how long I can continue imposing on Audrey's employers—I've been sleeping on a cot in her room."

"You may stay here, and Audrey is welcome to visit you, of course," Chicken Nancy said.

"That is very kind of you," Molly said. "Thank you."

I would never have said anything, but I felt a little relieved. I liked Molly very much, but rooming with a dwerg had drawbacks. She didn't seem to need a lot of sleep and was very active at night, bouncing around the room and climbing the bookshelves while humming and making sound effects with her mouth, usually explosions, motorcycles, and creaking doors. Of course, now that she wasn't crazy maybe those things would have stopped, but I was satisfied that she accepted Chicken Nancy's invitation.

CHAPTER 17

Questions

I was about to ask Chicken Nancy about the picture of Elizabeth Van Vreemdeling, with the cat whiskers, but Professor Tag got his question in first

"We first thought of coming to see you because we had some funny experiences with Spookhuizen," he said.

"The Van Vreemdeling mansion," Chicken Nancy corrected him. "It was never called Spookhuizen, which means 'haunted house,' when people lived there."

"The Van Vreemdeling mansion," Professor Tag said. "It doesn't seem to behave like a well-behaved house ought to behave."

"Let me guess," Chicken Nancy said. "When you tried to approach it, it moved away from you."

"It did!"

"And it may have even disappeared and reappeared."

"Only Audrey noticed it doing that," Professor Tag said.

"Perfectly normal," Chicken Nancy said. "Nothing to be concerned about."

"Perfectly normal? For a house to move around, and become invisible?"

"Not normal for a house," Chicken Nancy said. "If a house behaved like that it would be highly unusual to say the least. But that about which you ask is not a house."

"Not a house?"

"Not."

"If not, then what?"

"It is complicated to explain."

"I am a professor. I can understand anything," Professor Tag said.

"Of course. But I want the children to understand too, so you will forgive me if I use an example to illustrate."

"Certainly."

Chicken Nancy handed Professor Tag an object. "What do you take this to be?" she asked him.

The professor held the object, which was flat, about the size of a saucer, and reddish in color. "It is heavy. It is hard. It is smooth." He dug into his rucksack and produced a magnifying glass, and looked through it. "It has a complicated pattern of colors, predominantly a dark brownish red, and also lighter reds, touches of yellow, orange, blue-green, and black or very dark brown. Parts of it are very light and slightly translucent. I would take this to be a combination of various minerals, including iron, copper, possibly cobalt, manganese oxides, and quartz. The pattern suggests the structure of vegetation, or the grain of wood. So, I would take this to be a sample of petrified wood."

"That is correct," Chicken Nancy said. "I got it in Arizona in 1905. Now, can you tell me what petrified wood is?"

"Yes, I can," Professor Tag said. "It is wood turned to stone. It is a type of fossil. Wood becomes buried under sediment, because of a flood or some other natural occurrence. The wood is preserved from rotting away because of a lack of oxygen. Mineral-rich water flowing through the sediment deposits minerals in the cells of the wood, and as the cellulose and chemicals that compose the wood decay away, the minerals retain the exact form and appearance it originally had."

"So is what you hold in your hand a piece of wood?"

"No, it is a piece of stone."

"But it has the exact appearance of a piece of wood?"

"Yes."

"And it is identical to an actual piece of wood that once existed?"

"Certainly."

"Where is that piece of wood?"

"It is gone. It no longer exists."

"Now, if instead of handing it to you I showed you a photograph of it, what would you think it was?"

"Piece of wood."

"It looks exactly like a piece of wood?"

"Exactly."

"But it is not wood, not in any way except for its form and appearance?"

"Are you telling us that Spookhuizen, or the Van Vreemdeling mansion, is a petrified house?"

"Sort of. There was a house, but it is gone. Not a bit of it remains. But every bit of it has been replaced with something else," Chicken Nancy said.

"But not stone," Professor Tag said.

"Not stone."

"So what we saw is a sort of fossil house, but not petrified, not turned into stone," Professor Tag said. "It is turned into something else, but what?"

"What do you know about the house from your own observation?" Chicken Nancy asked.

"It looks like a house. The girls say they saw the flying saucers, or whatever they are, seem to enter it, or join with it in some way. And it moves about, seemingly in response to things in its vicinity, such as us trying to approach it."

"What category of thing moves about?" Chicken Nancy asked.

"Living things?"

"Have a Dutch cookie," Chicken Nancy said.

"It's alive?" the professor asked, munching a cookie.

"Can you think of a better explanation?" Chicken Nancy asked.

CHAPTER 18

Quick!

So instead of a living or once-living thing becoming a nonliving, mineral thing as in the process of petrification . . ." Professor Tag said.

"Assuming mineral things are nonliving," Chicken Nancy said.

"You are suggesting that a nonliving thing, such as a house . . ."

"Assuming houses are nonliving."

". . . has changed in every detail to a living thing that has the exact same form and appearance, only it is alive and it can even move around."

"Yes."

"Well, as crazy as I am, and have been, man and

boy for more than forty years, that is one of the craziest ideas I have ever heard."

"And yet it has a ring of truth to it, does it not?" Chicken Nancy said.

"I must admit, it does . . . for some reason," the professor said.

The professor and Chicken Nancy fell silent. It seemed they were both thinking about the phenomenon of the reverse-petrified house. I was thinking about asking Chicken Nancy about the picture of the cat-whiskered girl, but Weer began to bark, loudly and urgently.

Chicken Nancy sprang to her feet. She reached into an iron kettle and brought out a handful of thick, greasy-looking cigars.

"Quick! Everyone, take one of these cheap cigars and light it! Then run outside and puff smoke everywhere!"

"But . . . but . . . none of us smokes!" I said.

"It doesn't matter," Chicken Nancy said. "Here are kitchen matches. Just light one end and suck on the other—then blow the smoke out. Blow it everywhere! Hurry! Hurry outside! Get your cigars going! I will explain everything later."

Something that came as no surprise to me was that it was just about impossible to disobey Chicken

Nancy when she told you to do something. I ran out-side with the others. The cigar caught fire easily, and I sucked and puffed mouthfuls of smoke. It smelled like something between burning toast and tarpaper, and it tasted awful.

"Blow the smoke everywhere!" Chicken Nancy said. She was puffing a cigar herself. The clearing around the little cottage was filling with clouds of stinking blue smoke. Weer was running in circles, barking wildly.

It wasn't long before I began to feel sick. Molly was quite green. The professor was slightly green. Even Chicken Nancy was a little greenish.

"I think we can stop now," she said. "Thanks for your help."

I was dizzy. Things were swimming. I sat down on the ground. The professor was leaning against a tree. Molly had a disturbing expression on her face, and disappeared behind a bush.

"You said you would explain," the professor said. "Will you do that now?"

"Yes," said Chicken Nancy, who was not look-ing so well herself. "He can make himself invisible, or nearly invisible. You can see him against a thick fog—or smoke. If we had gotten outside in time and puffed enough smoke, it would have caused him to show up. Weer is a sort of sensor—he heard him or sensed him—I don't know how he does it. But apparently he had moved on before we got the smokescreen going."

"He? Who?" the professor asked.

"The Muffin Man."

"The Muffin Man?"

"Yes. Do you know the Muffin Man?"

CHAPTER 19

Yes, I Know the Muffin Man

Do you mean the local legend or local mythical Muffin Man?" Professor Tag asked. "The one who is said to live in Dreary Lane?"

"So you have heard of him," Chicken Nancy said.

"It is believed he was Matthias Krenzer, the old Dutch censor," Professor Tag said. "He stole the censer from the Old Dutch Church."

"Yes, that is the one."

"After stealing the censer, he lost his position as censor and became the town cleanser, cleansing the sidewalks and the steps of houses."

"You are indeed a learned fellow," Chicken Nancy said. "Yes, Matthias Krenzer, the old Dutch censor, who stole the censer, and became an old Dutch cleanser, later opened a small muffinery and became known as the Muffin Man."

"And Weer, the dog, is an old Dutch censor and cleanser sensor?" the professor asked.

"What's a censer?" I asked.

"Thing you burn incense in," Molly said. "They use them in churches."

"But as I understand it, Matthias Krenzer lived a couple hundred years ago."

"You understand correctly," Chicken Nancy said.

"And he is still around?"

"It would appear so."

"That would make him an extremely old person," I said.

"Or a ghost or something," Molly said

"Or something," Chicken Nancy said. "By the way, Molly, how are you feeling?"

"Pretty sane, I think," Molly said. "It feels a little strange."

"Wouldn't you like to go get your things and then come back here before it gets dark?" Chicken Nancy asked. "I don't want you wandering around at night with the Muffin Man in the neighborhood."

"Okay," Molly said. "I have a bag and a couple of things in Audrey's room at the bookshop. I'll go get them. Audrey, you want to come with me?"

"Before I find out more about the Muffin Man and other things?" I asked.

"I can explain all that later," Chicken Nancy said. "If you like, you are welcome to come back with Molly and stay for a while. Be sure to tell the Gleybners where you'll be."

"I can help Molly carry her things," I said. "Let's go now."

"In that case, I will go too," Professor Tag said. "I want to have my hat blocked. I will come back to hear the explanations another time."

We said goodbye to Chicken Nancy and Weer, and headed for downtown Poughkeepsie.

CHAPTER 20

Do You or Do You Not Know the Muffin Man?

We walked back toward downtown Poughkeepsie with Professor Tag.

"So, are you really not crazy anymore?" I asked Molly. "Did one cup of Chicken Nancy's special tea cure you?"

"I think so," Molly said. "But it's hard to put into words, or even feelings. I mean, I have been crazy so long, and when you're crazy you aren't noticing that you're crazy all the time—besides, I wasn't crazy every single minute, as you must have noticed. You know what it's like? It's like having forgotten something, and knowing you've forgotten something, only you don't know what it is you've forgotten, obviously, because you've forgotten it. Only, of course, in this case I am not trying to remember it. So let's change the subject."

"I'm happy for you, of course," Professor Tag said. "But, speaking for myself, not being crazy would make me sad."

"I was a little sad when I was crazy, and I'm noticing that I am not sad at all now," Molly said.

"Then Chicken Nancy did the right thing."

"What else do you know about the Muffin Man?" I asked the professor.

"Well, mainly I know the song and the game we played as children. We would sing, 'Do you know the Muffin Man?' and the adults would steal the muffins from our lunchboxes. Muffins were popular treats when I was a child."

"And at the end of the game, the adults would give the muffins back," I said.

"I don't remember them doing that," the professor said. "I was under the impression they kept them and ate them. Anyway, I did not know the Muffin Man was still around. We thought he was long dead."

"Apparently he is still around," I said.

"And invisible, even," Molly said. "And sort of evil or dangerous, from the way Chicken Nancy was acting."

"I want to hear all about him," I said. "And even more, I want to hear about that picture Chicken Nancy has."

"The one of you," Molly said.

"It's not me," I said. "It's Elizabeth Van Vreemdcling, Cornelius Van Vreemdeling's granddaughter and a friend of Chicken Nancy's mother."

"It's a picture of you," Molly said.

"Because of the whiskers?"

"Because of everything," Molly said. "Professor, you know that picture Chicken Nancy showed us?"

"The one of Audrey?"

"Yes, that one. Of whom is it a portrait?"

"Of whom? Of Audrey, of course," the professor said.

"She said! She plainly said it is a picture of Elizabeth Van Vreemdeling!" I said. "Why and how would she have an old oil painting of me, and why would she tell us it was of someone other than me?"

"You'd have to ask her that," the professor said. "At the very least there's a striking similarity. And here we are at the bookstore, and my goodness, look what a crowd!"

CHAPTER 21

They Are Among Us

There was quite a crowd. They were milling about in front of the UFO Bookshop, and there were a lot of people inside. I recognized most of them—they were regular customers. But what were they all doing here at once?

Molly and I threaded our way through the press of people and went inside the shop. Mrs. Gleybner saw us and hurried toward us. "Oh, you're just in time, girls!" she said. "Put on these aprons and start handing around apple cider and cookies. We have an important guest. He will be arriving any moment."

We put on the aprons and carried trays with little paper cups of cider and sugar cookies and offered them to the people. It turned out the important guest was Eland I. Tankwiper. He was an author, and he was coming to the bookstore to sign copies of his book, *They Are Among Us*. It was all about how aliens from space are here on Earth and living disguised as regular Earth people. Eland I. Tankwiper was a specialist in subjects such as space aliens. I had read parts of the book. We had a copy in the store. It claimed that Woodrow Wilson, Johann Sebastian Bach, Walt Disney, and Josef Stalin were all residents of other planets who had come to live on Earth. Now there was a whole box of copies of *They Are Among Us,* and lots of copies stacked in a pyramid in the window.

The people all applauded when Tankwiper arrived. He had on a beautiful blue suit, and a long flowing mustache. Mr. and Mrs. Gleybner shook hands with him. They stood around for a while, laughing and smiling and chatting. Then Mrs. Gleybner caught sight of me and motioned for me to come toward her. I knew what was coming.

"We have a surprise for you, Mr. Tankwiper," Mrs. Gleybner said. "I don't suppose you thought you would meet a real extraterrestrial in a bookshop here in Poughkeepsie. This is Audrey, our very own space alien."

Eland I. Tankwiper pulled a pair of horn-rimmed eyeglasses out of his breast pocket and put them on.

He peered at me through the glasses, took them off and cleaned them with his handkerchief, and put them on again. Then he put his glasses back in his pocket and said, "I regret to contradict you, Mr. and Mrs. Gleybner, but this young lady is not an extraterrestrial. If you refer to the illustrations in the back of my book showing the various types of space aliens, you will find there is not one that looks like her. She is nothing but a common or garden variety Earth girl with a set of whiskers. Very nice whiskers, to be sure, but she is nothing out of the ordinary."

The Gleybners were crestfallen. They did their best to hide it, but I could see that Eland I. Tankwiper had spoiled one of their favorite imaginary beliefs. I had long before stopped trying to explain that I was not a space alien—it seemed to make them so happy to believe I was.

So I took offense at what Tankwiper had said. First of all, it was impolite of him to disappoint the Gleybners like that. And I didn't care for his saying I was nothing out of the ordinary. I wondered how many people he had met who came from another plane of existence, not to mention someone extraordinary enough that a wise woman more than a hundred years old had an oil painting of someone who looked enough like her that her friends thought it *was* her.

Mr. Tankwiper sat at a little table, and the people lined up to have their books signed. Molly and I continued to pass around the cider and cookies. Everyone seemed to be having a good time, but I took a dim view of the whole business. When I got a chance I whispered to Mrs. Gleybner, "Just because he wrote a book does not mean he knows everything."

"Do not worry yourself," Mrs. Gleybner said. "We have authors here quite often, and we are used to them."

CHAPTER 22

Horse?

By the time all the books had been signed and all the people had departed and Mr. Tankwiper had left with his pockets stuffed with cookies, it was already late afternoon.

"It will be getting dark by the time we get to Chicken Nancy's house," I said. "Maybe we should stay here tonight, and go in the morning."

"She is expecting us," Molly said. "And we can't very well telephone her to say we're not coming. If we walk fast, we can get there before nightfall."

"She was particular that she didn't want us wandering around after dark."

"So we won't. Let's tell Mrs. Gleybner, and start out right away."

Of course, carrying Molly's things slowed us down a bit. And then there was the runaway horse.

We were on the street that turned into a semi-country road and led to the place where we would turn the corner at the Christmas tree farm. By this time the sun was low in the sky, but it looked to Molly as though we would make it in plenty of time —when the horse came along. It was an old horse, pale gray, almost white, and wrinkly around the nose, with dull, old-looking eyes, and it shuffled along as though it didn't have much energy. It had a green halter on and was dragging a length of rope.

"It looks like this horse has gotten away from somewhere," Molly said. She grabbed the rope. The horse came to a stop and rested its chin on her shoulder. "Nice horsie," she said, stroking his old nose. "Give him something."

I had some leftover cookies from the bookstore in a paper bag in my pocket. I fished one out and gave it to the horse. He ate it.

"Give him another," Molly said.

The horse wound up eating all the cookies. I was going to give them to Chicken Nancy, but they were storebought cookies, and not very good compared to the ones she baked. The horse thought they were swell.

"What now?" I asked. "We can't just stand here in the street, feeding this horse cookies all day."

"Obviously he has gotten loose from somewhere," Molly said. "We should find out where he belongs."

"How do we do that?" I asked. "Does he have a little tag around his neck, or a horse license?"

"That's dogs," Molly said. "I don't think horses have those."

We were walking now, the horse shambling along with us, probably hoping I had more cookies. "We should ask people if they know where he comes from."

"There's nobody around," I said. "People are in their houses, preparing supper."

"Well, look for someplace farmy-looking," Molly said. "We'll knock on the door."

"What if they don't know?" I asked.

"Well, we can't just leave him in the road. He might get in a collision with a car. He doesn't look very bright. I guess we can just take him with us to Chicken Nancy's. You want to ride him?"

"I don't know how," I said.

"Just haul yourself up onto his back," Molly said. "And I'll lead him."

I put my arms around the horse's neck and scrambled onto his back. I got the feeling he didn't mind it.

Molly handed her bags up to me and I lay them across his sharp backbone in front of me.

"Comfy?" she asked.

"Somewhat," I said. "Why are we doing this?"

"Well, for one thing, I was getting tired of carrying the bags," Molly said. "And you can see farther from up there. See anyone looking like belonging to the horse?"

"There is someone way up the street," I said. "He's coming this way."

"Let's go meet him," Molly said. "With luck, it will be the horse's owner."

In a few minutes we saw a kid. The kid saw us and began to run toward us. He was a big, strapping, muscular kid in overalls and big boots. He had unruly sandy hair and freckles. All he needed was a straw hat—the perfect picture of a farmboy.

"Diablo! You found Diablo!" the kid shouted. "Thank you!"

"What did he do, run away?" Molly asked.

"More like wandered away," the kid said. "Old as he is, he can hop over the fence, and sometimes he just takes off, strolling. Usually, I find him eating grass near his paddock. This is the farthest he has ever gone."

"Do you live on a farm around here?" I asked.

"No, I live in an apartment house about a mile away," the kid said. "Diablo lives on a farm—or what's left of a farm—up the road and you make a left. Nobody lives there—the house burned down—but there is a shed where Diablo lives, and a little fenced area. I hike over two or three times a day to take care of him."

"What is your name?" Molly asked.

"Call me Jack," the kid said.

"Well, we have to be on our way, Jack," Molly said. "Glad we could help with Diablo."

"Where are you going?" Jack asked.

"Christmas tree farm."

"That's on my way!" Jack said. "Would you like to ride with your friend? Get up on Diablo. He can carry both of you. I'll lead him."

Jack lifted Molly onto the horse as if she weighed nothing, settled her behind me, took hold of the rope, and led the horse.

As I suspected, riding on Diablo was a good deal slower than walking, but it would have been too complicated to explain to Jack that we didn't want to ride once we were already on the horse. Besides, Jack was cute.

"So you live in an apartment and take care of this horse," I said. "What is that all about?"

"I always wanted a horse," Jack said. "When

Diablo's farm burned down, the farmer was going to send him to be dog food, so I asked if I could have him. I have to carry bales of hay on my back from the feed store up the road, and I carry buckets of water from the gas station. He takes up so much of my time and energy that I'm flunking out of high school."

"It is worth it?"

"Totally."

We arrived at the corner and the Christmas tree farm.

"I really appreciate your catching Diablo for me," Jack said after we slid down off the horse's back. "If there is ever anything I can do for you, just come a little way past the Christmas tree farm. You can't miss Diablo's paddock and shed—it's the crummiest thing on the whole road. If I'm not there when you come, I will be soon. And, it's none of my business, but why are you going to the Christmas tree farm when it's almost dark? The place is haunted like nobody's business."

"We have a friend who lives nearby," I said.

"And ghosts don't scare us," Molly said.

Not only was it almost dark, but a fog had rolled in. Everything was gray and murky-looking. Jack said goodbye to us and led Diablo away. They were swallowed up in the murk in half a minute, and we started along the driveway.

"Well, we got here before night—sort of," Molly said.

"Did you mean it when you said ghosts don't scare us?" I asked Molly.

"Sure I meant it."

"Good—because this is the ghostiest-looking place ever."

CHAPTER 23

In the Fog

It was hard to tell what was shadow and what was solid object in the fog. It was one of those greenish, greasy fogs, and when we were twenty paces into the Christmas tree farm we had no way to tell where we were. Only by continuing to walk in the direction we'd started could we have even a vague clue that we were heading the right way.

We didn't talk. By the time we reached the point at which we couldn't tell if we were still in the Christmas tree farm or had reached the woods, I realized we were holding hands. Then Molly spoke.

"Do you smell something?"

"You mean like—?"

"Like muffins."

"Yes."

"It can't be, can it?"

Of course, it could, and was—a sweet muffiny smell, the smell you would get if you opened a bag of muffins and stuck your nose in. And there was a thick, darker place in the fog ahead of us—ahead and above—where there was something tall and . . . evil. My whiskers were tingling.

My mind was processing a lot of information that I was not getting from the usual senses—it wasn't something I saw or heard, or the muffin smell, that told me it was something evil. I was getting that from some part of my brain I hadn't known was there. But I was certain that something really bad was closing in on us, and from the way Molly was squeezing my hand, I could tell she was getting the same message.

"Why don't we stop walking?" I asked myself. And then I realized we had stopped—it was the patch of darkness that was moving . . . toward us, and getting darker, and bigger.

We never did see him clearly. He remained just a cloudy darkness, even when he spread himself and rushed us. I felt myself choking. Like choking on a muffin. We were being enveloped in the blackest black. There was no pain, but I was very sure the worst kind of pain was about to come. Molly screamed.

Well, she didn't exactly scream. It was like a scream, but also like a whistle, also like rattling pebbles in a can, also like breaking glass. It was the kind of sound that makes you see colors and flashes of light. And it wasn't a scream of fear. It was more like a weapon, a sharp knife.

And in that moment there were thousands, or hundreds of thousands, of sharp knives whizzing all around us. Fast-moving, making a keen, hard, singing noise, slicing and slashing—I knew these things could cut through anything, and I imagined the burning wounds and my hot blood spilling, but they were not touching us. They were after the big black foggy thing—and it was hurting. I saw, or felt, or maybe heard it twist and shift, recoil and jump, trying to collect itself so it could get away. But they were after it, the thin, quick, vicious things. And all the time, Molly was screaming that ear-breaking scream.

Then the scream stopped. The sharp, angry flying things stopped. The black thing was gone. And here was Chicken Nancy, holding up a lantern and carrying an old-fashioned blunderbuss. Weer, the dog, was with her.

"Well, I see I had no call to worry about you," she said. "You're quite the dwerg, Molly dear."

"Chicken Nancy! You saved us!" I said.

"Not I," Chicken Nancy said. "Though I did bring my blunderbuss loaded with rock salt and juniper berries."

"Would that have worked?" I asked.

"Well, he wouldn't have liked it," Chicken Nancy said. We were walking along now. "But what Molly did was much more effective. I doubt he'll be back this way for a year or more after that experience."

"What exactly did I do?" Molly asked.

"It was your dwergish instinct," Chicken Nancy said. "You called out the tree spirits to protect you."

"The tree spirits?"

"Oh, yes. Every Christmas tree has a fierce, bloodthirsty demon within it," Chicken Nancy said. "And people think all they risk by bringing them indoors is burning the house down."

CHAPTER 24

What Happened?

We were sitting at Chicken Nancy's table. She had cut us thick slices of hot apple pie with crumbly cheddar cheese on top, and poured glasses of milk from a crockery pitcher. There was a fire in the kitchen fireplace, and the room was lit by candles. Weer was sleeping by the fire. We felt so cozy and safe in the little house that being scared to death in the fog seemed like it had happened a long time ago.

"What happened out there?" Molly asked.

"You ran into the Muffin Man," Chicken Nancy said.

"We figured that out," Molly said. "But the other things that happened. Tree spirits, you said. What was that all about?"

"You summoned them," Chicken Nancy said.

"How could I have summoned them? I never heard of them before."

"It was instinct," Chicken Nancy said. "Dwergs have powers."

"They do? The only power I noticed dwergs having when I was living at home was the power to stay on their feet after drinking lots of homemade Catskill Mountain gin."

"Are you sure?" Chicken Nancy asked. "Have you never noticed any powers?"

"You mean like knowing things about people before they tell me, and knowing what they are thinking?"

"For example," Chicken Nancy said.

"I thought that was just part of being crazy. Isn't it?"

"What am I thinking right now?" Chicken Nancy asked.

"You are thinking it's a pity I didn't come along sooner so you could set me straight."

"I am. But it's not too late. And by the way, remember how you used to be crazy?"

"Sure, until you cured me with that special tea."

"That was Lipton's from the store. You were never really crazy to begin with. It's just that nobody ever explained things to you. You just needed to stop thinking you were crazy. I hope you will forgive my little deception."

I have to admit, I felt a little jealous. Chicken Nancy was so nice to Molly. I wished I thought I was crazy or needed to have things explained to me too.

"Oh, you're just as mixed up as I am," Molly said to me. "There's plenty you don't understand."

"Oh, yes, the mind-reading thing," I said. "Well, I would like to know about that picture."

"The one of you?" Molly asked.

"The one of Elizabeth Van Vreemdeling," I said. "It's not me."

"Well, there is a striking resemblance," Chicken Nancy said. She had gotten the picture out of the drawer, and we looked at it. In the candlelight, it looked real and alive, and exactly like me.

"That's because it's you," Molly said.

"I don't know why you keep saying that," I said.

"Because it's a picture of you," Molly said.

"Look, unless Chicken Nancy is playing an elaborate joke on me . . ."

"Which I would never do," Chicken Nancy said.

". . . then it is a portrait of a girl who lived well over a century ago."

"And yet you and she are one and the same," Molly said.

"And you think this because?"

"Because look at the evidence," Molly said. "Here is the picture, and here are you, right in front of me."

"Besides my having absolutely no recollection of being Elizabeth Van Vreemdeling, how do you account for the fact that if I were she, I would be older than Chicken Nancy?"

"How old are you, anyway?" Molly asked.

"It's a funny thing," I said. "I don't exactly know. Fourteen, fifteen, somewhere in my teens. You see, Uncle Father Palabra, who raised me, is a retired monk, and even though he is retired he spends a fair amount of time in prayer or being silent, meditating and the like. I always assumed that was why he never told me a lot about my own history. He has various monkish ways about him. For example, we never celebrated our birth-days—instead, we would celebrate the birthdays of Saint Pussycat, who has nine per year."

"Saint Pussycat?"

"A saint Uncle Father likes especially. I'm not sure if she is an official saint. My earliest memory is of reading about Saint Pussycat in one of Uncle Father's books."

Molly was grinning. "So you don't know your right age, and the first thing you can remember hap-pened when you were already able to read."

"I see where you're going with this," I said. "And while I don't know my *exact* age, I think it is pretty obvious that I am not over a hundred years old, so I am obviously not Elizabeth Van Vreemdeling."

"It's not terribly likely," Chicken Nancy said. "But I wouldn't rule it out completely. It is more likely that you are her doppelgänger."

"What's a doppelgänger?"

"Person who is exactly like you," Chicken Nancy said. "Some people believe each of us has one. Maybe Elizabeth Van Vreemdeling is yours."

"Who was she exactly?" Molly asked Chicken Nancy. "Tell us about her."

CHAPTER 25

Elizabeth's Story

Cups of tea, I think," Chicken Nancy said. "And then I will tell you what I know about Elizabeth Van Vreemdeling, and after that I think it will be time for us to sleep." Chicken Nancy poured out cups of tea. We sat at the table, sipping and listening, with Weer snoring at our feet.

"First, Elizabeth Van Vreemdeling was not actually a member of the family. She just turned up at Spookhuizen under mysterious circumstances and wound up adopted."

"What were the mysterious circumstances?"

"It was said that she had come in a flying saucer."

"They knew about the flying saucers back then?" I asked.

"More so than now," Chicken Nancy said. "There

was more flying saucer activity in the nineteenth century than there is today. People had a lot of theories about them, and there were books written and articles in the press. Even Mr. Lincoln used to tell a story about flying saucers."

"Abraham Lincoln?"

"Yes. He told a story about a flying saucer that landed in New York City and broke a wheel. The captain of the flying saucer went into the nearest open shop, which happened to be a bagel shop.

"'Give me one of those flying saucer wheels,' the saucer captain said.

"'Those are not wheels,' the shopkeeper said. 'They are bagels.'

"'Bagels?' the saucer captain said. 'What are bagels? What do you do with them?'

"'We eat them,' the shopkeeper said. 'Here, try one.' He handed the saucer captain a bagel.

"The flying saucer captain took a bite of the bagel. 'Not bad,' the saucer captain said. 'You know what would go well with this?'

"'What?' the shopkeeper asked.

"'Lox, and cream cheese,' the space man said."

"Abraham Lincoln told that story?"

"Abraham Lincoln knew about lox and cream cheese?"

"And flying saucers?"

"Well, he told a lot of stories," Chicken Nancy said. "And he was president of the United States, so he knew about everything, lox and cream cheese included. As to knowing about flying saucers, some think he came from another planet himself."

"I love history," Molly said. "It's my favorite subject. But what about Elizabeth? Do you know more about her?"

"My mother said she was a nice girl, kind and pleasant, and aside from her special powers, normal in every way."

"Her special powers?"

"Yes, she seemed to know when the flying saucers were going to appear, and some thought she could communicate with them—but the really unusual thing about her was that she seemed to have some kind of relationship with the Wolluf."

"The Wolluf?" I asked.

Weer whimpered under the table.

"The Wolluf is a rare animal," Chicken Nancy said. "Either it is the last great wolf here in the Hudson Valley, or it is supernatural—maybe a werewolf. It is almost never seen, and very large and wild. People were very much afraid of it."

"You said it *is*—present tense," Molly said. "It doesn't still exist, does it?"

"Some say it doesn't—those who remember it at all," Chicken Nancy said. "I say it does. There are a lot of stories about it, including the belief that anyone who sees it will go mad. Of course that is not true—I saw it once when I was a young girl, and nothing happened to me. I was frightened, of course, but it didn't cause me to lose my mind. Anyway, Elizabeth Van Vreemdeling was quite chummy with it, and for that reason people feared her and thought she was a witch."

"You saw the Wolluf?" I asked. "What was it like?"

"Well, let's say that compared to seeing the Wolluf, meeting the Muffin Man is like a birthday party," Chicken Nancy said. "I see you have finished your tea. Pass your cups to me and I will read the leaves."

"Read the leaves?"

"At the bottom of your cup, the little fragments of tea leaves will have made a pattern. I can tell what they mean."

I looked into my cup. I didn't need Chicken Nancy to tell me what the pattern meant. It was more of a picture than a pattern—a shaggy, scary, four-footed picture. I passed her the cup and she looked into it.

"Oh, my," she said. "What a coincidence. The Wolluf."

"What do my tea leaves say?" Molly asked.

"Another coincidence," Chicken Nancy said. "A castle."

"Why is that a coincidence?"

"Because the only castle around here is on Pollepel Island, and Pollepel Island is said to be the best place to run into the Wolluf."

CHAPTER 26

Destiny

What became of Elizabeth Van Vreemdeling?" I asked.

"She disappeared one day," Chicken Nancy said. "Nobody knew where she went. Do you girls ever think about destiny?"

"Never," Molly said.

"I'm not sure I know what it is," I said.

"Me neither," Molly said. "That's why I never think of it. What is it?"

"One's fate," Chicken Nancy said. "A predetermined course of events over which one has no control. Something that is bound to happen to some purpose you know nothing about. For example, it is possible that the two of you were destined to meet in order that you carry out some task or participate in some happening, which is also destined."

"I don't know about that," I said. "On an impulse, I took a bus from one plane of existence to this one. I wound up in Los Angeles, stayed there awhile, and then hitched a ride to New York with an eccentric movie actor named Marlon. He was handsome and pleasant, but it got so I couldn't stand his playing the bongo drums, and his boring conversation, so I got out in Poughkeepsie, also on an impulse. Then I happened to meet Professor Tag, went to visit him at the nuthouse, where I happened to meet Molly, and we became friends."

"And I got away from my backward mountain-dwelling ancestors in the Catskill Mountains, made my way to Poughkeepsie, where I sort of lived in the streets, until I got picked up, diagnosed as crazy, and tossed in that same nuthouse. I don't remember a lot of the details, but that is because I myself thought I was crazy at the time, so I didn't bother to pay a lot of attention. I don't see how either of our stories sounds much like destiny," Molly said.

"You may be right, of course," Chicken Nancy said. "Or it may be that all those random events were leading you to a point you are both destined to reach."

"Do you think that is so because Audrey's tea

leaves showed the Wolluf and mine showed the castle?" Molly asked.

"Oh, I didn't say I thought so, or thought not-so," Chicken Nancy said. "I just asked if you girls ever thought about it. And now it is late."

"It's not more than eight p.m.," Molly said.

"We keep early hours in this house," Chicken Nancy said. "And you were only just cured of imaginary madness, and the two of you had an exciting encounter with the Muffin Man. You should rest. I will show you to your beds."

Chicken Nancy opened the door to a neat little room with two neat little beds with pretty quilts on them. The beds looked so inviting that I instantly began to feel sleepy.

"Go directly to sleep," Chicken Nancy said. "I will call you quite early in the morning, and tomorrow may be a strenuous day."

Molly was yawning too. Chicken Nancy left us with a single candle for light, and we undressed and got into the beds, which were extremely comfortable.

"I feel suddenly terribly tired," Molly said.

"So do I," I said.

"Blow out the candle."

It seemed no more than a minute after blowing out the candle before I fell into a deep sleep—but just as I did, I heard Chicken Nancy's footsteps, the scratching of Weer's claws on the brick floor, and the sound of a door opening and closing. For some reason I had a mental image of Chicken Nancy wearing a cloak, carrying her stick, Weer beside her, leaving the little house.

CHAPTER 27

A Giant

When we woke there was a smell of pancakes. We pulled on our clothes and hurried to the kitchen. Chicken Nancy was at the stove, making pancake after pancake, and sitting at the table, eating pancake after pancake, was a big shaggy thing. It had a huge head of greasy, matted hair, round shoulders, and big dirty hands with fingers thick like bananas, and it was wearing what might have been a coat and might have been a bathrobe—it was hard to tell through the grime. All I could make out of the face were two tiny bright eyes and a nose like a potato—the rest was beard.

"This is Harold," Chicken Nancy said. "Harold, as you see, is a Catskill Mountain giant." Harold mumbled something into his pancakes. "Sit down, have some pancakes, and get to know him." Harold patted his lips with the end of his beard.

"More pancakes," Harold said, and then, "Harold need to use toilet."

"It's out back, Harold dear," Chicken Nancy said.

When Harold stood up, I thought his head was going to brush the ceiling, but he was short! He was no taller than Professor Tag! "He's short!" I said to Chicken Nancy when he had left the room. "He's about five foot seven!"

"It's impolite to mention people's physical characteristics," Chicken Nancy said. "It's true, Harold is small for a giant, but he is a giant nonetheless, and from an ancient race of giants. And think of this, girls." Chicken Nancy was smiling. "Harold has a boat!"

"I see what you want!" I said. "You want us to go to that island!"

"Pollepel Island," Chicken Nancy said.

"Yes! Where the Wolluf is!" Molly said.

"Well, it may or may not be," Chicken Nancy said. "As to wanting you to go, I can't say I actually want you to go—I just thought you might be curious to go. It's a very interesting place. The native people would never go there. They thought it was an evil place and haunted. And the Dutch thought so too. They thought it was where the wild things were. After the Civil War, a man named Bannerman bought up all the old soldier hats, and bayonets, and cannons, and tons of leftover gunpowder, and built a rather ornate castle on the island to keep it all in."

"What did he do with it all?" Molly asked.

"He sold it to small armies in other countries, and collectors, and theatrical companies putting on plays. Also, all those cannons you see on courthouse steps and town squares came from there. After a while he died and his sons moved their war-surplus business to Brooklyn and stopped using the island. It's been standing deserted for the past few years."

"So you think we would be curious to go to an island that the Indians thought was haunted—and evil—that the Dutch thought was haunted, and that is full of explosives, and apparently go there in a boat with a giant who must be the smallest . . ."

"Shhh!" Chicken Nancy put a finger to her lips.

Harold was back. "Harold want more pancakes," he said.

"I'm curious to go," Molly said.

"What? You want to go?"

"Well, yes. I think it would be interesting."

"What about the Wolluf? You want to see the Wolluf?"

"I especially want to see the Wolluf."

"Chicken Nancy says it's fierce. She says after seeing the Wolluf, meeting the Muffin Man is like a birthday party!"

"Are you scared?"

"No, I am not scared," I said.

"Then let's go, since you're not scared."

"Fine," I said. "We'll go."

"Harold take girls to island?" Harold asked.

"Yes," Chicken Nancy said. "And bring them back when they're done."

"Unless we get eaten by a Wolluf or something," I said.

"Harold protect girls," Harold said. "Harold has cudgel. See?"

Harold reached under Chicken Nancy's table and pulled out a big knotted club, which he waved about awkwardly.

"He has a cudgel. How nice," I said.

"You may as well get started," Chicken Nancy said. "I have packed you a picnic lunch." She produced a wicker picnic basket. "Harold will carry it. Do not eat the lunch all by yourself, Harold. Share it with the girls."

"Sandwiches?" Harold asked.

"Yes, lots of sandwiches," Chicken Nancy said. "Have a good time on the island."

CHAPTER 28

Oh, Hell

We go!" Harold said.

We followed him out of the little house. He walked a little ahead, carrying the picnic basket and swinging his cudgel. From behind he looked a little like a haystack—and really like a giant, from the way he stomped along, as long as there was nothing to compare his height with.

We passed through the woods, past the orchard and the Christmas tree farm, and along the road. We saw Diablo standing in his paddock, no doubt waiting for Jack to turn up with his morning hay. We passed little farms and houses, fields and bits of forest. After we crossed the road that led to the main entrance of the loony bin, our way began to slope downward toward the river.

Near the bank of the river Harold led us into a thicket. It was dense, and we had to push our way through some heavy underbrush. Harold pushed some bushes aside and dragged out something large and black and round.

"Oh, hell," I said. "It's a coracle."

"What's a coracle?" Molly said, looking at it.

"A coracle," I told Molly, "is the most primitive, and also worst, boat in the world. As you see, it is shaped like a bowl. It's made of branches with skins stretched over it, and it's waterproofed with a coating of tar."

"Why is it round like that?" Molly asked.

"As far as I know, it is because the people who invented it were not quite smart enough to figure out that a boat-shaped boat would work a lot better."

"Is good boat," Harold said.

"Prepare to be sick . . . and wet . . . if we have to go in that thing," I said.

"How come you know all about coracles?" Molly asked me.

"My uncle has one."

"Is it safe? Will we drown? Will we die?"

"Well, we won't drown, if Harold knows what he's doing. And even if he doesn't, I do. But if we're in the thing for very long you won't care if you drown. Harold, how far is it to this island?"

"Not far," Harold said. "Get in boat. We go."

Once we were in the coracle it all came back to me. I remembered how much I hated my uncle's one. Harold's was larger, and it bucketed and flipped and spun, also tilted wildly from side to side, and dipped forward and back. Harold stood and worked the oar, first on one side, then on the other. Each time he switched sides, the oar would drip water into the boat, so we were getting wet, being pitched about, and feeling sick.

"This is fairly disgusting," Molly said.

"I told you," I said. "But it's tolerable for a short trip. How soon will we get to the island?" I asked Harold.

"Not long," Harold said. "Five, six hours, maybe."

"Kill me now," Molly said.

CHAPTER 29

You Can Get Used to Anything, Almost

Harold was good at handling the boat. The big problem with a coracle is that you can't point it in a direction because it doesn't have a point. If you don't pay attention or stop working for a moment, it will just spin and bob, going nowhere. The Hudson has currents, and finally Harold found one—then all he had to do was steer, and the river carried us south at a pretty good clip. The boat didn't bounce and wobble as much.

It was a mild morning, and the view from the river was pretty. We stopped being nauseated and were almost comfortable, except when a barge or ship went past. Big oceangoing freighters and huge barges pushed by powerful tugboats go up and down the

Hudson, and they look really very big when you see them from water level. When one of them passed us it was like looking up at a moving mountain. Then the ship would glide beyond us and the river would feel very smooth for a minute . . . and then the water churned up by the ship's massive propellers would catch us. Wave after wave would shake us and cause the little boat to jump up and smack down again and again. It was a completely scary experience. Add to that, the ships would sound their horns when they saw us, and the noise made us temporarily deaf, so getting knocked around by the wake of the propellers would take place in silence.

"I may have miscalculated just a little," Harold said. "The trip may be longer than five or six hours."

Molly and I looked at each other.

"What happened to 'Harold have boat. Boat good. Harold good giant' and all that stuff?" Molly asked.

"Oh. Sorry. Harold make mistake. Trip take longer," Harold said.

"Forget the pidgin English," Molly said. "We know you can talk regular. Why the act?"

"Harold have inferiority complex," Harold began. "I mean, I . . . I do it beause I'm short for a giant. Talking like that sort of jacks me up a little. It sounds more gianty."

"So you're educated?"

"I have a degree from Vassar College."

"I thought it was a girls' school."

"They take a few males. They need them in the Dance Department, and in my case the Anthropology Department wanted to study me."

"Is that what you studied, anthropology?"

"I majored in classical accountancy," Harold said.

"And Professor Tag was your teacher," I said. "That makes sense."

"My senior project was about double-entry book-keeping in the age of Pericles," Harold said.

"What were you saying about miscalculating, speaking of people who are good with numbers?" Molly asked.

"Oh, yes, that," Harold said. "Remember when I said it would take five or six hours to get to the island?"

"Yes."

"Well, if that had been correct, we'd have arrived around noon. But I got mixed up. Comes of trying to figure in my head using roman numerals."

"And now that you've thought it over?"

"We'll get there more like midnight," Harold said.

"Oh, goodie! More time in this stinking coracle!"

"Well, I could put in at that little island over there and you could get out for a while and stretch your legs," Harold said. "Would you like me to do that?"

"I don't know about Audrey," Molly said. "But I was just thinking I would whack you with your own cudgel if you didn't."

CHAPTER 30

On the Island

I call dibs on going behind that bush first," Molly said.

"I'm next," I said.

"I'll start unpacking the lunch," Harold said.

It was a small, rocky island, not much bigger than an average backyard. There was a nice patch of soft grass with a few little trees around it, and there we sat and ate the sandwiches Chicken Nancy had packed— goat cheese on crusty bread with thin slices of sweet onion. There was also a bottle of lemonade, and some thick, crumbly sugar cookies. The sun warmed the grass, and we lay on our backs, shading our eyes with our hands.

"Remind me," I said to Molly. "Why are we making this trip?"

"Because Chicken Nancy wanted us to make it."

"But she never said why."

"She's wise. She's a wise woman. What's the point of knowing someone like that if you don't do what she tells you?"

"I always do what she tells me," Harold said. "Those old wise women can throw a mean curse if you make them mad."

"I don't think Chicken Nancy would curse anybody," I said.

"I take no chances," Harold said.

"But why did she send us?" I said. "That's what I would like to know."

"Well, obviously she thinks it's destiny, or maybe your destiny," Molly said.

"Not yours?"

"Maybe mine, but I think yours."

CHAPTER 31

Pirate Pete's

When we got back into the coracle, it didn't seem as horrible as it had before lunch. We were used to it. We'd gotten our sea legs, or more accurately our sea bottoms, since all we had to do was sit. Harold had equipped the boat with a couple of water bottles, so we could take a drink, and an umbrella, which we used to keep the sun off. The bouncing and rocking didn't bother us anymore, and we even dozed off at times and napped our way down the river.

Harold paddled like a true giant. He never seemed to get tired. But he did get hungry. So did we. "Time for supper!" he said, and turned the little boat in toward shore.

There were four or five old barges, huge things made of massive tarred timbers like squared-off tree trunks. They were tied together with hunks of thick rope, and partially beached on what looked like a mud flat. "This is where we can get something to eat," Harold said.

He tied up the coracle to the side of one of the hulking barges, and we scrambled up a ladder. Then we had to go from barge to barge on shaky plank walkways.

"These are old railway barges," Harold told us. "People bought them for one hundred dollars apiece when the railroad was through with them."

"What did they do with them?" I asked.

"They lived on them," Harold said. "Back during the Depression, when nobody had any money. There used to be a lot more of them—it was like a little town. Now just Pirate Pete lives here, and he runs a speakeasy and restaurant."

"What's a speakeasy?" Molly asked.

"At the time, the sale of alcohol was made illegal," Harold said. "So these illegal bars sprang up. Speakeasies, they were called. Pirate Pete's is probably the only one left, now that there is no more Prohibition law."

There was a sort of house built on Pirate Pete's barge, with a regular house roof, and windows, and a chimney with smoke coming out. We went inside and saw it was all one big room, with tables and chairs and a big bar, and there were clusters of green wine bottles with round bottoms hanging from the ceiling. Inside each wine bottle was a wire with a tiny light bulb. They cast a weird green light that made the whole place seem like it was under water. There was a big painting of a mermaid behind the bar, and there were fishnets with cork floats hanging on the walls. It was a neat place.

Pirate Pete was a little, greasy-looking guy with no hair, and no eyebrows, and I think he had no eyelashes. "Why, it's Harold the giant! Welcome to Pirate Pete's," he said.

"Harold hungry," Harold said, reverting to his giant-talk. "Girls hungry. We want food."

"I have smoked eel sandwiches and home-fried potatoes," Pirate Pete said. "Beer for the giant, and ginger ale for the girls."

"Bring food," Harold said. "Harold has money. Harold will pay."

There was a stack of smoked eels, looking stiff, on a platter on the bar. Big things, they had fierce faces, but they smelled sort of yummy. The smoked eel sandwiches were on big football-shaped rolls, freshly baked. I had never tasted smoked eel before. It was excellent, and the home-fried potatoes were perfect.

"Pirate Pete catches the eels right here in the Hudson River," Harold told us. "And he smokes them himself. It's not the cleanest river, as you may have noticed—but just this once won't hurt us." Then to Pirate Pete he said, "Harold want more. Bring more eels. Bring more beer. Then bring apple pie and coffee."

The apple pie and coffee were even better than the eel sandwiches, and went well with the setting sun, which we watched through the windows.

"Okay! Enough eating! Here is money!" Harold paid Pirate Pete. "Now we go back on river."

"Come again," Pirate Pete said.

Making our way along the shaky gangplanks was even scarier now that it was almost dark. We climbed down the ladder into the coracle, and headed out into the river.

CHAPTER 32

Night

The river was quiet at night. There wasn't much traffic, and we passed a number of big freighters and barges at anchor. Most of the time, the only sound we heard was Harold's paddle hitting the water. Then there was a tremendous splash. "That's river sturgeon jumping," Harold told us. "They can get to be as long as fifteen feet, and weigh eight hundred pounds. They jump clear out of the water, and to answer the question forming in your minds, if one of them fell on the boat, it would probably be the end of us."

"Fifteen feet?" Molly asked.

"Well, not all of them get to be that big. There are sharks in the river too, from time to time."

"Sharks? In a river? Don't they prefer salt water?"

"The Hudson is what you call a riverine estuary," Harold said. "It's salty, or brackish, all the way up to Poughkeepsie, and it has tides, like the ocean."

There was another splash. It sounded close.

"How often do those sturgeon jump into boats?" I asked.

"It hardly ever happens," Harold said. "It has never happened in all my time on the river."

"How long has that been?"

"Let me see. I bought the coracle about a year ago, and then I had to spend some time fixing it up, so . . . six months?"

Molly and I sat quietly. Harold paddled. After a while, he began to sing.

"Loudly the bell in the old tower rings,
Bidding us list to the warning it brings: Sailor
    take care,
Danger is near thee, beware, beware, beware,
    beware—
Many brave hearts are asleep in the deep, so
    beware, beware.
Many brave hearts are asleep in the deep, so
    beware, beware."

"How jolly," I said.

"He has a nice voice for a giant," Molly said.

He started another song.

"Wasn't it sad when the great ship went down?
Wasn't it sad when the great ship went down?
Uncles and aunts, little children, lost their pants.
It was sad when that great ship went down."

The moon got high. It was almost full, and very bright. It cast a beautiful light on the river. Molly and I looked around, hoping to see a sturgeon jumping, preferably not too close, but it never happened.

"Look! You can see the castle!" Harold said.

Far down the river, we could see the moonlight glinting off something—it was hard to say if it was a castle. As we got closer, it did start to look like a castle, a weird, extra-fancy one with all kinds of turrets and towers and decorations. All the windows were dark, and it looked about twenty times spookier than Spookhuizen.

"That's it? That's where Chicken Nancy wants us to go?"

"No, we said we wanted to go," Molly said. "She said maybe we wanted to go, and we said we did."

"Right, and the night before, she went out while

·· 140 ··

we were sleeping to hunt up a giant with a boat, and bring him home," I said.

"Don't let first impressions prejudice you," Harold said. "You may have a lot of fun there."

"Oh, I can see it's a million laughs," I said.

"You don't want me to row you all the way back without even looking it over, do you?" Harold asked.

"No, we'll take our chances," Molly said.

"Great," Harold said. "Because I am never going to make a trip this long in this crappy boat again."

"What? How did you plan to get us back?"

"Well, I figured when you were through on the island, I'd put you on a bus."

"Bus? What bus?"

"Right over there," Harold said, pointing to the shore. "You can catch a bus. It takes about half an hour to get to Poughkeepsie."

"Wait a minute! So we could have taken a bus down this far in half an hour?"

"Maybe forty minutes."

"And then just rowed out to the island? In a rented rowboat or something?"

"Well, yes, I suppose so. But then you would have missed the whole trip on the river," Harold said. "We have to stop talking now. These currents are really tricky, and I need to pay attention."

The currents *were* tricky. We shot right past the island.

"Drat!" Harold said. "This isn't easy. Now I have to turn the boat around."

Harold was struggling with his paddle. The coracle was trying to spin. Twice he almost managed to get us back to the island, and then the current got the better of him and carried us downriver.

"I think I have to go way over toward the other shore and sort of swing around and come up to the island on the west side," Harold said. "I never saw such crazy water."

It turns out that in addition to the castle, which was really just a warehouse for old cannons, gunpowder, army shoes, cooking pots, and swords and such, Mr. Bannerman had built a mansion to live in. When Harold finally managed to get close to the island, we saw it, and a big stone arch over the water, which he was able to paddle through. There was a sort of stone patio or dock right in front of the mansion with a set of steps leading up to it. Harold caught ahold of a big iron ring and held the coracle close to the steps.

"Okay, girls, up the steps you go," he said.

"Up the steps we do not go!" I said. "Do you see what is standing in front of the mansion?"

Standing in front of the mansion, on a sort of veranda lit by a couple of torches in iron brackets, were four or five monsters taking the air, their thumbs tucked into their waistbands! They all had fat bellies, and big heads, and a couple of them had horns; all but one had a wide mouth with lots of sharp little teeth, and the one that hadn't had a beak like a parrot's and feathers growing out of the top of its head. They all had big feet with claws. A couple of them were smoking pipes. Their expressions were not unpleasant, but they were monsters! They could afford to look friendly.

"So? What is the problem?" Harold asked.

"You ask what is the problem? There are wild things right in front of you, and you want to know what the problem is?"

"Well, you must have expected there would be something unusual on the island," Harold said.

"Of course we did," Molly said.

"What? And you want to go visit them?"

"Well, maybe not without permission," Molly said. Then she shouted, "Hey! Monsters! Is it okay for us to come ashore?"

"You're the kid who scared off the Muffin Man!" one of the monsters shouted. "Sure, come ahead! We won't bite you!" Then all the monsters laughed. I wished they hadn't done that.

"Wow, that only happened last night, and already they know about it," Molly said. The monsters were all gesturing and beckoning us to come to them.

"And you're Elizabeth Van Vreemdeling!" one of the monsters said. "Also known as Audrey from another existential plane."

"That's it. I'm going ashore," I said. "There's destiny going on."

Molly and I scrambled up the ladder.

"Have a good time, girls!" Harold said while pushing off in the coracle.

"What? You're not coming with us?"

"Not me," Harold said. "I've visited here before."

"Is that Harold in the boat?" one of the monsters asked. "Yah, yah, Harold! You're scared to come in because you lost your pants playing klabiash with us last time!"

"I'm going to paddle down to Yonkers and catch an all-night movie," Harold said. "I'll come back tomorrow and see if you're ready to leave."

"Yah, yah, Harold is scared! Some giant!" the monsters called.

"Wait!" I called to Harold. "Are we safe here?"

"As long as you don't play for money, you're safe," Harold said, and the coracle disappeared into the darkness.

"We would never play for money against children," one of the monsters mumbled. "Do you have any money, girls?"

"Not a cent," Molly said.

"Me neither," I lied. I had twenty-six dollars pinned to my underwear.

CHAPTER 33

We Play Cards with Monsters

The monsters were Hudson River trolls. Their names were Phil, Fay, Helen, Joe, and Uncle Bernard. We thought that Helen and Joe were the children of Phil and Fay, and Uncle Bernard was their uncle. They were all the same size and appeared to be the same age. Hudson River trolls live four or five hundred years. They believe they are descended from sasquatches that lived on the Esopus Creek. They didn't explain the reason that Uncle Bernard looked like he was part bird and the others looked like they were part bear or part gorilla or part buffalo—and there didn't seem to be a polite way to ask about it.

They lived in the mansion on Pollepel Island, which is also called Bannerman's Island. They said they were looking after it for the Bannerman family, should they ever decide to come back, and besides, it was deserted and would have gone to waste if nobody lived there.

The trolls loved to gamble and would place bets on whether the castle, which was half full of gunpowder, would blow up the next time lightning hit it. And they kept us up until two in the morning playing klabiash.

The trolls were answering no questions and would discuss nothing until we had played klabiash with them —so there was nothing to do but play.

Klabiash is a card game. Their other favorite game is filthy euchre, but they thought klabiash would be easier for us to learn. The dealer gives each player three cards, face-down, until the thirteenth card, which is dealt face-up. Then the players grab cards, throw cards down, and shout things like "Menell!" "Yass!" "Deece!" and "Shmice!" Yass is worth twenty points, Menell is worth fourteen points, and when anybody calls Shmice, they throw the cards in the air and run around the room, jumping over furniture. The game ends when everybody is sweaty and exhausted. The trolls said we were good players, even though we had no idea what we were doing.

"Time for you to sleep," Phil said. "Go upstairs. There are thirteen bedrooms—take any one or ones you like. We will have pea soup and Danish pastries for breakfast."

The bedroom we chose was simultaneously fancy, old, and crummy. It must have been the height of fashion when Mr. Bannerman built the place in the 1880s, but it had plenty of time to get out of date, and we were not surprised to find that the trolls were not careful housekeepers. We pulled the dusty bedspread off the big old bed, which was made of dark wood, carved all over, and had a canopy. The sheets seemed reasonably clean, and there were no mice in the bed. We were tired after a day on the river and the energetic game of klabiash, so we climbed in and fell asleep in a minute.

Molly must have been really tired. She slept all night and did not climb the drapes or do sound effects of the Battle of Britain with her mouth, or practice tap dancing. In fact, she was still asleep when I woke up early in the morning. I dressed and went downstairs. The trolls were sleeping in too, so I played with a cute frisky puppy I met in the parlor until the rest of the house woke up.

CHAPTER 34

With the Trolls Before Breakfast

The puppy scampered off somewhere, and the trolls came thundering down the stairs with Molly bouncing after them.

"Breakfast!" Helen called. "Split-pea soup and Danish pastries! And who wants prune juice?"

"Me! Me! Me! Me!" Phil, Joe, Fay, and Uncle Bernard shouted.

Helen got busy in the kitchen, and soon the old mansion was full of good smells that did not go together.

"After breakfast, we can play cards!" Joe said.

"Or we can talk with our guests," Uncle Bernard said. "What brings you to our island, girls?"

"Well, do you know Chicken Nancy?" I asked.

"The wise woman? Of course we know her," Fay said. "We've known her since she was born."

"Chicken Nancy suggested we come here," I said.

"She was telling us about the Wolluf," Molly said. "And she said this was the best place to see it."

When Molly mentioned the Wolluf, the trolls went pale and gasped. There was a little period of silence. Then Uncle Bernard spoke slowly. "Great pineapple, preserve us! You *want* to see the Wolluf?"

"Well, yes," Molly said. "We're curious."

"Most people would rather run a mile than see the Wolluf," Fay said.

"We see it all the time," Joe said. "And we are big strong trolls, brave as anything, and afraid of nothing—and even we have to get ahold of ourselves to keep from losing our prune juice."

"Is it horrible?" Molly asked.

"It is worse than horrible," Phil said.

"Is it evil?" Molly said.

"Not so much evil as frightening," Fay said. "It's the kind of thing you can hardly bear to look at. I would rather see a half-dozen regular werewolves than look at the Wolluf. And yet you dare not look away."

"Of course, that would not apply to little Elizabeth here," Uncle Bernard said. "She has never had a problem with the Wolluf—and she is the only one of whom that can be said."

"Yes, the Wolluf is the scariest thing in the whole valley," Joe said. "By the way, its name is Max."

"Max?" Molly asked.

"Max."

"That's a funny name for something so scary."

"I doubt you will think it's funny when you see it."

"By the way, I am not Elizabeth Van Vreemdeling," I said. "My name is Audrey, and I come from another plane of existence."

"How adorable. She doesn't know who she is," Uncle Bernard said.

"I certainly do know who I am," I said. "And I never heard of Elizabeth Van Vreemdeling until the other day."

"Then how do you account for the fact that you are she?" Uncle Bernard asked.

"I don't know that I have to account for it," I said. "First, I am not she, have no recollection of being her, never heard of her, and besides, she lived a long time ago."

"So did we," Uncle Bernard said. "And yet here we are, us."

"But, I assume you have always been you," I said.

"More or less," Uncle Bernard said. "But then, all of us are any number of people as we go along, if you'd care to think about it. I mean, once you were a baby, quite different from the girl you are now, and later you will be an adult, also different. Can you remember being a little baby?"

"No."

"But you do not deny you ever were such a thing as a baby, do you?"

"Well, no."

"Why not, since you don't have any recollection of being one?"

"Because everyone starts out as one."

"And how do you know that is so?"

"How do I know everyone starts out as a baby?"

"Yes. What makes you think that is so?"

"Observation?"

"Oh, so you have observed every single person starting out as a little infant and growing up to be a child, an adolescent, and an adult?"

"No, not *personally* observed."

"Then why do you think it is true?"

"Because everyone knows it."

"So, you believe it because there is a consensus of opinion about it."

"Yes."

"Excellent," Uncle Bernard said. "Everyone who believes Audrey here is Elizabeth Van Vreemdeling, raise your paw."

All the trolls raised their hands, Helen called from the kitchen, "I believe it," and I saw that Molly had raised her hand too.

"It seems we have a consensus of opinion," Uncle Bernard said.

"That is not proof," I said. "You could all be wrong. I might just look a lot like her."

"You have a point," Uncle Bernard said. "Nothing is ever definite, but you have to admit there is more of a possibility that you are Elizabeth than you previously thought."

"Maybe a tiny bit more," I said. "But I am far from convinced."

"What would convince you?"

"Nothing I can think of, unless I suddenly remembered being Elizabeth, which I do not."

Molly said, "You all say that Elizabeth Van Vreemdeling had a different reaction to the Wolluf from everyone else. I would be interested in seeing if Audrey does too, besides being interested in seeing the Wolluf."

"Well, it's before breakfast, but I suppose we could call him if you think you want to see him on an empty stomach," Uncle Bernard said. "And as I think about it, that might be the best way."

"You can just call him and he will come?"

"Yes, but we tend not to."

CHAPTER 35

The Wolluf

All right. You asked for it," Joe said. He put two fingers in his mouth and whistled loudly. "Max!" he shouted.

I noticed all the trolls were shading their eyes with their hands. Molly looked excited. I braced myself for something ghastly. I heard the scrabbling of claws and the thumping of paws. I heard raspy panting.

And then . . .

CHAPTER 36

Breakfast with a Wolluf

The puppy, the one I had been playing with earlier, came bounding into the room. He headed straight for me. I sank to my knees and hugged and petted him. He put his paws on my shoulders and licked my face. At first I thought I was protecting him from the Wolluf, and then I realized that nothing else was about to enter the room.

While this was happening, the trolls were moaning and groaning.

"Oh, lordy, how terrible! How frightening! How unbearable!"

Molly was saying similar things, but she wasn't groaning. She was clapping her hands, and jumping up and down.

"What is all this? What is so horrible? What are you seeing that you find so unpleasant?" I asked the trolls.

"Unpleasant? Painful is more like it," the trolls said.

"Molly, what are you seeing?"

"Oh, it is bad," Molly said. "I mean, it is scary. I'm not seeing anything. It's like there is nothing to see. There's . . . there's a hole in reality. It is like absolute darkness—only it is so dark, it's bright. It's like looking at the sun, if the sun were the source of all darkness."

"And it pulses. And coruscates. And flashes blackness," the trolls said. "It is like staring into the pit of hell. As often as we see it, it never gets easier."

"I would rather be stuffed in a garbage can and thrown down a well than look at this," Joe said.

"I would rather be put through an industrial olive-pitting machine than look at this," Fay said.

"I would rather be trampled to death by a hundred elephants than look at this," Phil said.

"I would rather die, be reborn as a skunk, and then be stepped on by a moose than look at this," Helen shouted from the kitchen.

"What are you seeing?" Molly asked me.

"Cute puppy," I said.

"Cute cute, or horrifying and diabolically cute?"

"Regular cute," I said. "He likes me. What happens if I wrap him in my sweater?" I put my sweater around the puppy and held him.

"A little better," Uncle Bernard said. "Still scary, but better."

"Would you like to take Max out on the veranda while we have our breakfast?" Helen asked. "Molly can bring yours outside to you."

"I'm not sure I can eat," Joe said.

CHAPTER 37

Away from the Island

I shared my Danish pastries with Max. He wasn't interested in the split-pea soup. Neither was I.

"This is confusing," I said to Max. "Do you think I might actually be Elizabeth Van Vreemdeling?"

"Obviously you're Elizabeth," Max said.

"You can talk! How is it you can talk?" I asked.

"I'm the Wolluf," Max said.

"And you too think I am Elizabeth."

"Not think—know," Max said. "I'm the Wolluf. I'm never wrong about things like this."

"Is that why Chicken Nancy arranged for me to come here, so you could tell me I am Elizabeth Van Vreemdeling? Which I still do not believe, by the way."

"I would imagine she wanted you to meet me because I am the only one who can guide you where you have to go," Max said.

"And where do I have to go?" I asked the Wolluf.

"Let's leave that for later," Max said. "Are you ready to take a little trip with me?"

Molly had come out onto the veranda.

"Can Molly come along?" I asked.

"I see no reason why not," the Wolluf said.

"We going somewhere?" Molly asked.

"Max wants to guide me," I said. "Are you up for it? Is he still looking terrifying to you?"

"Pretty terrifying—but I am learning to deal with it," Molly said. "These Hudson River trolls may be four hundred years old and know a lot, but they don't have nerve like a Catskill Mountain dwerg."

"Good girl," Max said. "I don't do it on purpose, you know."

"It talks," Molly said.

"I was about to mention that," I said.

"So what do we do first?"

"First we get off the island and ashore. You girls strong swimmers?"

"Not with these currents," I said. "Besides, I think I see Harold the giant making his way upstream. He can take us across."

Molly leaned in through the open door and called to the trolls, "We're going soon. Would it be all right with you if we took the Wolluf away with us?"

"All right?" the trolls answered all at once. "We would love it, and be grateful forever."

"In that case, we'll be pushing off with Harold before long," Molly said. "Thanks for the breakfast and the bed and the klabiash game and everything."

"Would you mind if we didn't come out to see you off?" Uncle Bernard said. "It's just that looking at the Wolluf one last time might make us sad."

"Or sick," Molly said. "Do you have a big bag of some kind?"

"Like how big?"

"Big enough for a large puppy, I guess," Molly said.

"How about a Spanish-American War knapsack? We have one of those for carrying firewood."

"Toss it out here, and we'll try it for size," Molly said. To Max she said, "What do you think? Can you fit in this?"

"I think so," Max said. "What's the idea?"

"It's so Harold the giant doesn't jump out of the boat when we put you in," Molly said.

"Oh! Good thinking," Max said.

Harold was working his way closer.

"Come get us off this island!" I shouted to him.

"Fershlugginer currents!" Harold shouted. "I'm doing the best I can."

On the third try, Harold managed to get the coracle up against the dock.

"Be careful with this," Molly said as we handed down the Wolluf.

"What is it?" Harold asked.

"Talking knapsack. Don't open it."

The trolls had stuck their arms out various windows and were waving handkerchiefs.

"Goodbye, trolls! Thanks for everything!" we shouted, and stepped into the boat.

Harold pushed out into the current. "So what's in the bag?" he asked.

"Would you believe . . . the Wolluf?" Max asked.

"Holy pineapple!" Harold said.

CHAPTER 38

Harold, Row the Boat Ashore

Do you mean to tell me you caught the Wolluf?" Harold asked.

"Not caught," Max said. "I can bust out of this rucksack anytime I want."

"We just thought it would be better not to distract you," Molly said.

"I'm fairly distracted," Harold said. "You do realize that the Wolluf is the most terrifying and powerful supernatural thing in the whole valley, do you not?"

"Ha! And that is without half trying," Max said from inside the bag.

"I think he's cute," I said.

"But given that every normal person, and also dwergs, trolls, and I don't know what else, finds him unbearable to look at and scary to the point of fainting or throwing up, or both, we thought it would be best to conceal him so you could work the boat without getting everybody drowned," Molly said.

"I have a strong inclination to head for shore," Harold said. "Was that what you wanted me to do?"

"Yes," Max said. "Make with the paddles."

We helped Harold drag the coracle out of the river. He chained it to a sapling with a bicycle chain and lock, and we covered it with branches.

"What now?" Harold asked.

"I'm coming out of the bag," Max said.

"Do you have to?" Harold asked.

"Just close your eyes tight," Max said. "Nobody is asking you to look."

"I'll just take a tiny peek," Harold said. "Ack! That's enough."

"Sissy!" Max said. Then to Molly and me, "It's too awkward for me to travel with you in daylight and a populated area. Let's meet somewhere after dark. Can you get to Poughkeepsie from here?"

"Harold says there's a bus," I said.

"Fine. I'll meet you outside the old lady's house when it gets good and dark."

"But she said she was frightened when she saw you," I said.

"Well, you can warn her not to look outside. Anyway, it will be just the three of us."

I was petting Max's cute head. He still looked like a puppy to me. Molly was forcing herself to look at him, but there were tears streaming down her cheeks. She looked as though she had been slicing onions. Harold had tears streaming down his cheeks too, though his eyes were closed tight.

"Okay, I am going to disappear now," Max said. "I'll see you tonight."

"He's gone," I told Harold.

"I need to lie down," Harold said. "But first I'll show you where to catch the bus."

"You're not coming with us?"

"No. I'm going to see if I can sell the coracle. And then I am going to check in to a cave somewhere and try to sleep off the glimpse I had of that Wolluf."

CHAPTER 39

Fuss on the Bus

On the bus, Molly went to summing up. "Let's see . . . the trolls think you're Elizabeth Van Vreemdeling; the Wolluf, who seems to be the most important supernaturalnik in the valley, thinks so; I think so; Professor Tag thinks you probably are; and Chicken Nancy doesn't say you are and doesn't say you aren't but thinks you shouldn't rule out the possibility. I'm wondering if maybe you're ready to change your vote."

"Look," I said. "You can't take a poll and convince me that I am someone I know I am not just because a certain number of people believe I am. It doesn't work that way. I know I am not Elizabeth . . . If I were, I would know it. To me that makes perfect sense."

"So you're saying you know you are not Elizabeth Van Vreemdeling because you just know it—no reason, just know. Is that right?"

"Of course. How does anybody know they are who they are?"

"It's an interesting question. What if everybody you knew and everybody you *ever* knew called you Susie Bunny Booboo? What would you think then?"

"I'd think it was a gag—they were all doing it on purpose."

"Or?"

"That they were all crazy."

"Or?"

"That I was crazy. Do you think I am crazy?"

"Not at all, and I am in a position to be able to tell. But don't you think it is just possible that if absolutely everyone called you Susie Bunny Booboo that it might be your name."

"Well, for the sake of argument, it might be possible, but it isn't my name. I am not Susie Bunny Booboo, and I am not Elizabeth Van Vreemdeling."

"You are not because . . . ?"

"Because that is not my name."

"And what is your name?"

"You know my name. My name is Audrey."

"Audrey what? What is your second name?"

"It's funny. I never had a second name. Or I never knew one."

"So all you know is your first name. Your second name could be anything at all?"

"I suppose so."

"Could it be Van Vreemdeling?"

"It could, but you are just playing games with my brain. It could be Bunny Booboo just as well."

"I'm just trying to point out that you can't say you know that you aren't Elizabeth Van Vreemdeling—you just feel you have no reason to believe that you are."

"That's almost the same thing."

"Almost, but not quite."

"Look. I happen to resemble someone who lived around here a long time ago. Why would that make people think I was that person—who is probably dead a long time ago—except that everyone who thinks so is extremely weird—no offense."

"None taken. And you neglect to mention that this long-ago Elizabeth Van Vreemdeling was also connected with the flying saucers in some way, and was the only person who didn't mind looking at the Wolluf, and in fact got along with him. And also you more than resemble her—you look exactly like that portrait Chicken Nancy has. I am not insisting you are the very same person—though I have a feeling you are—but you have to admit it is more than a casual likeness."

"Well, that far I am prepared to go."

"Fine. I just ask you to keep an open mind, is all."

CHAPTER 40

Mousetrap Soup

The bus took us within a block of the bookshop. We spent the day helping Mrs. Gleybner with unpacking boxes, dusting books, feeding the cat, and drinking tea. As evening came on, we set out with a box of cookies from Mrs. Gleybner for Chicken Nancy.

When we got to Chicken Nancy's little house in the woods, Professor Tag was visiting. They were making mousetrap soup.

"Hello, girls! Back already?" Chicken Nancy said. "How was your trip? Did you learn anything interesting? Is Harold with you?"

"Harold is somewhere downriver trying to sell his horrible coracle," I said.

"The trip was fine," Molly said. "We quit throwing up after a few hours. And we ate eels."

"We went to Pollepel Island, and stayed overnight, and played klabiash with trolls," I said.

"We came back on the bus," Molly said. "And we made friends with the Wolluf. His name is Max, and he's meeting us here tonight."

"Did you say the Wolluf?" Professor Tag asked. "I'll be going now. I just remembered there's a sale on birdseed at Mega-Mart." He grabbed his hat and rushed out the door.

"When you say the Wolluf is coming here . . ." Chicken Nancy said.

"We're meeting him outside," I said. "He'll understand if you stay in the house so you don't have to look at him."

"Explain to him that I'm an old woman," Chicken Nancy said.

"It will be fine," Molly said.

"He's not evil or dangerous, you know," I said.

"I know," Chicken Nancy said. "But he's painful to look at, and even if you try you can't actually see him."

"Audrey says he looks like a cute puppy," Molly said. "I can look at him, because I have incredible willpower, but all I see is that intense eye-hurting darkness. And of course there's the feeling of terror, nausea, and being suffocated. But he doesn't do it on purpose."

"I am glad to know the Wolluf is nice, personally," Chicken Nancy said. "But unless it is absolutely necessary, I will forgo the pleasure of meeting him. Meanwhile, this mousetrap soup is ready. Let's try it out."

CHAPTER 41

Cloaks

We ate mousetrap soup and told Chicken Nancy about the trolls, and what the house on the island was like, and Pirate Pete's. All the while it was getting darker and darker.

When it was fairly dark but not fully dark, Chicken Nancy went into a closet and brought out two cloaks. They were gray and made of a lumpy and irregular kind of cloth. They were long, and had hoods. We tried them on. They looked to me like cloaks worn by the old Dutch in colonial times, as shown in the wall paintings at the Poughkeepsie post office.

"You may need them," Chicken Nancy said.

"It's a mild night," I said.

"Just the same, take them along," Chicken Nancy said.

"They look old fashioned," I said.

"They are old," Chicken Nancy said. "I got them from my mother. I don't know which cloak, but guess who one of them belonged to."

"Elizabeth Van Vreemdeling!" Molly said.

We folded the cloaks over our arms. "I suppose we should go out and wait for Max," I said.

"I will go to bed, and I will lock the dog in with me," Chicken Nancy said. "Have a nice visit with the frightening monster."

CHAPTER 42

On a Smooth Stone

The Wolluf was already there when we came outside.

"Ah, here you are! And you have cloaks. Good. Now, why don't the two of you sit on this smooth stone. I will walk up and down and caper about while I tell you things you do not know."

Molly and I sat on the smooth stone. The Wolluf, appearing as a cute puppy to me, and as a horrifying darkness to Molly, walked in circles, hopped up onto a stump at times, and talked to us.

"You understand, this is about destiny," the Wolluf said. "All this stuff that's been happening to you is mainly about Elizabeth's destiny—maybe a little bit yours, Molly—but mainly Elizabeth's."

"I know just about everybody thinks I am Elizabeth Van Vreemdeling," I said. "But I don't buy it, mainly because if I were she, I'd know about it. Wouldn't I?"

"Maybe you would, and maybe you wouldn't," the Wolluf said. "Are you familiar with the concept of alternate planes of existence?"

"I come from another plane of existence," I said.

"She comes from another plane of existence," Molly said.

"So you understand that it's a little as though we were all living on a single floor of a multistory apartment building, only we're completely unaware of the existence of the other floors."

"I explained all that at the beginning," I said. "What about it?"

"Well, this about it," the Wolluf said. "In addition to there being simultaneous activity on different planes, have you ever considered that there might also be activity on different temporal planes?"

"You mean in addition to stuff going on at the same time on different planes of existence, there is stuff going on in the past and future on other planes that are separated from one another by time instead of . . . whatever the planes we already know about are separated by?" Molly asked.

"Right," the Wolluf said. "So if you imagine the planes that are simultaneous as being stacked on top of one another, like the floors in an apartment house—and it is sometimes possible to get a glimpse, or actually shift from one floor to another, as Elizabeth, or Audrey, has done—you can also imagine shifting to the planes that are ahead or behind us in time. You follow?"

"Sure," Molly said. "There are lots of complete worlds out there we know nothing about, and the inhabitants of which know nothing about us, some in the same time continuum, and some ahead of us or behind us in time."

"Usually," the Wolluf said.

"Usually," Molly said.

"I'm not done yet," the Wolluf said. "Now imagine that in addition to the different floors of the imaginary apartment house, there are cellars, crawlspaces, attics, storage rooms, garages, sheds, secret passages, and hidden staircases."

"Oh, boy!" Molly said.

"And they are full of people?" I asked.

"Some are, some aren't: some are full of other-than-people. Some are in the same time-space continuum as others, some are in different ones, and some are not all one thing or all another."

"What do you mean by that?"

"Well, you know that there are parts of Pough-keepsie that are not city, not suburb, not country, not industrial, not wasteland, and maybe not solid land and not water. You might have a little cottage, a place that makes truck tires, a drugstore, a field of corn, a pond, a woods, a swamp, and the police station, all within sight of one another."

"Yes. So?"

"So imagine there was an existential plane sort of between this one we are now on and the next one—sort of an unofficial mishmash of a plane, not one thing and not another, not now and not then. Can you imagine something like that?"

"Yes. Why do you want us to?"

"Because I want us to go there."

"Does it have a name? Also, why?"

"It is called Apokeepsing, and I want us to go there so Elizabeth can maybe meet herself. Anyway, something like that."

"Are you following this?" I asked Molly.

"After a fashion," she said. "Are you?"

"More or less," I said. "I'm not sure it matters. Maybe the Wolluf isn't expressing it clearly, or maybe he doesn't know what he's talking about."

"But you want to go to this demiplane, mishmash place."

"Oh, definitely," I said.

CHAPTER 43

Take the Cloaks

So how do we get to this where-or-whatever-or-when-ever-it-is?" I asked.

"Be here at dawn," the Wolluf said. "Bring the cloaks—you'll definitely need those. Give the old lady my regards, and tell her you don't know how long you'll be gone." Then he vanished.

We tried not to make any noise going to bed, but Chicken Nancy heard us. "Wolluf gone?" she called from her bedroom.

"Gone for now," we called back to her. "He'll be back at dawn. We're going somewhere with him and we don't know how long we'll be gone."

"Take the cloaks with you," Chicken Nancy

called. "And there are lunches for you and the Wolluf in paper bags on the sideboard. Have a nice time."

"Do you think she knows where we're going?" I asked Molly.

"I think she knows what the Wolluf eats for lunch," Molly said.

"Do you think she's really afraid to see him?"

"I don't know. Maybe they were boyfriend and girlfriend, or boy monster and girl witch, in 1850, and broke up on bad terms," Molly said. "Maybe they are secretly in cahoots and are cooperating to arrange our destiny. I do know that I have the feeling everybody around here knows more about what's going to happen to us than we do."

"I have the same feeling," I said. "It's as though we are characters in a story somebody else is writing."

CHAPTER 44

A Sinking Feeling

When we stumbled outside at the crack of dawn, the Wolluf was waiting for us.

"Is that lunch?" the Wolluf asked. "What did she pack for us?"

"I think it's cold fishcake sandwiches," I said.

"My favorite! She makes the best fishcakes of anyone," the Wolluf said.

Molly and I looked at each other. Why would the Wolluf know a thing like that?

"Now let's get started," the Wolluf said. "Stand over here, side by side."

We stood on a little bare patch of ground. The Wolluf scurried around, bringing pebbles and twigs and carefully arranging them on the ground in some

complicated pattern. While he did this, he sang a song
under his breath.

"... to Honky-Tonky Town.
It's underneath the ground,
where all the fun is found.
There are singing waiters,
syncin' syncopaters,
and a jazz pianna played by Mr. Brown.

"All right, now start walking around each other,
counterclockwise, and when I tell you, stamp your
feet hard.

"... *he plays it all by ear—*
the music that you hear
will make you stay a year.

"Now stamp your feet as you walk! Stamp! Stamp!
Stamp!

"*He's even got the monkey*
dancin' with the donkey
down in Honky-Tonky Town."

It is next to impossible to describe what it feels
like to be swallowed up by the earth—in fact, it is not

next to impossible; it is impossible. It is even impossible to contemplate it while it is happening. The best I can do is say we were swallowed up by the earth. Swallowed up and spat out again. It was too unexpected to be scary, and happened too fast for us to know if it was uncomfortable—but I know it wasn't comfortable. All I can tell for sure is that one moment we were sort of circling each other counterclockwise and stamping our feet in the woods outside Chicken Nancy's house, and in another moment we were doing the same thing, only going clockwise, someplace else.

"You may stop now, girls," the Wolluf said. "We have arrived."

CHAPTER 45

But Where?

It was the Wolluf talking, but the cute puppy was nowhere to be seen. Molly was not seeing the uncomfortable-making brilliant darkness. The only person near us who was not us had to be the Wolluf—besides, the bulky man wearing clunky boots, baggy trousers, and a long-sleeved shirt buttoned up to the neck was speaking in the Wolluf's voice. He had very pale skin, yellow eyes, pointy teeth, long hair, and whiskers all over his face—he was handsome in a scary way.

"You changed," I said.

"I do that—especially during a full moon. And so have you," the Wolluf said. "Have a look at yourself."

My hand, holding the bags of lunch, was covered with lovely soft orangey fur. When I pushed my sleeve up, I saw that my arm was furry too, and stripey with alternating reddish and yellowish stripes. My cheeks felt fuzzy.

"How do I look?" I asked Molly.

"Much more pussycat-ish," Molly said. "It's a good look for you. How about me? Anything different?"

I looked Molly over. "You still look like you, only maybe a foot taller, and you sort of remind me of Chicken Nancy now—something about the look in your eyes."

"You'd best put your cloak on, Audrey-Elizabeth," the Wolluf said. "And you too, Molly—just so we all look like a group from the same period."

"Is this what you actually look like?" I asked the Wolluf.

"It is at present," the Wolluf said. "Same as it is with you. Now take a look around and tell me where you think we are."

"It's a lot like downtown Poughkeepsie," I said. "Is it Poughkeepsie?"

"I recognize some buildings," Molly said. "But they look a little different."

"It smells different too," I said. "I smell woodfires, and coal, and horses—and is that cough drops?"

"Also, some of the people are unlike the citizens of Poughkeepsie as we have come to know them," Molly said. "For example, there are many of what seem to be lizards, walking upright and wearing old-fashioned clothing, and birdlike people. Also regular humans, or something close to it."

"So what gives?" I asked the Wolluf. "Where are we, and what is the nature of this place?"

"Well, as I was explaining to you, this is a sort of quasi-existential plane. It is squished in between the plane on which Poughkeepsie as you know it exists and some other plane of a more stable nature, and has attributes of both, plus qualities of its own. We are neither here nor there, and that goes for time as well as space. Feel free to ask questions."

"I have a question," I said. "That building with the golden statue of a chicken on top—unless I am mistaken, it is very much like the building I have visited many times as the site of the Panopticon Theatre, a popular movie house. But as I see it now, it has no marquee and no box office, and instead has an ornate set of doors with another golden chicken above them. Can you explain how and why it is different?"

"Certainly," the Wolluf said. "The building as you have known it contains a movie theater, but a hundred years earlier it was the Temple of the Mystic Brotherhood, a popular secret society or lodge to which many prominent citizens of Poughkeepsie belonged in the early and mid-nineteenth century. The golden chicken is their insignia."

"So is it a hundred years earlier here?" I asked the Wolluf.

"In places," the Wolluf said.

"In places?" I asked.

"Time is unstable here," the Wolluf said. "The building is as it was a hundred or more years before you knew it in Poughkeepsie, but here in Apokeepsing, it may be much older than that, or it may exist in the future. And the building next to it, which is a Portuguese bakery in your time, might be of a whole different time period, older, newer, not built yet, or long ago collapsed into a heap of dust."

"And the building next to that, which is designed to look like a gigantic green pepper. Where does that come from, time-and-space-wise?"

"I have no idea," the Wolluf said. "And to add to the confusion, since this is an unstable plane, what you are seeing now may be changed, or not here, or mean something else tomorrow."

"In other words, a mishmash," Molly said.

"I believe that was how I described it," the Wolluf said.

"I have done comparatively little television-watching in my young life," Molly said. "Since my early days were off with the dwergs of the mountains, and I didn't have a regular home, really, until I landed at the loony bin—and there, of course, the TV is on all the time—but I am sure I have seen fifty stories with a premise just like this."

"Well, of course," the Wolluf said. "They love to make those because they can reuse sets and scenery from other shows . . . and let's say they have half enough cowboy costumes, and half enough Nazi costumes. They just write a script about a world where there are Nazis and cowboys. It's a cheap device used in movies too. Pretty soon fiction writers will start using it in books."

"So why did you bring us here?" I asked. "Not that it isn't very interesting."

"I thought I would show you something in the Temple of the Mystic Brotherhood," the Wolluf said. "They have a sort of museum of antiquities and curiosities there."

"Okay, let's go in," I said.

"It's not as easy as that," the Wolluf said. "Only members may enter, and they are really strict about it."

"But you're the Wolluf. You can do anything, right?"

"It's true I have powers on the plane we just came from—but here I have them and I don't. It's best not to try to do anything fancy. To enter the temple, we'd need to get permission from Baas Kwaadwillig."

"Who's that?"

"Baas Kwaadwillig is the master of the Mystic Brotherhood. He also runs the town—call him the mayor, or the dictator. And he is dangerous and evil."

"Very dangerous?"

"And very evil. It is believed he does bad things to people."

"What sort?"

"All sorts. Male, female, young, old, human, otherwise—he makes no distinctions."

"I meant what sort of bad things."

"Oh, very bad. Bad as can be."

CHAPTER 46

Neither Here nor There

Take a look. There he goes now," the Wolluf said.

We saw a man who was all angles. It was as though none of his knees or elbows, ankles or wrists, worked in the usual way. He was dressed all in black, with a black high hat, and he was walking like a double-jointed crab, bent over, with the aid of a crooked stick. He had pale gray skin, long, straight gray hair, a wiggly pointed nose and little dark pinpoint eyes. Baas Kwaadwillig looked over his shoulder, fixed us with a pinpoint gaze that made me think of stale shredded wheat and moldy prunes, and went into the Temple of the Mystic Brotherhood.

"What do you think of Baas Kwaadwillig?" the Wolluf asked.

"He looks as bad as can be," I said. "Are we going to ask him for permission to enter the temple?"

"Possibly not at this time," the Wolluf said. "It might be better to look around and get better acquainted with our surroundings first."

"Let's take a walk," Molly said.

Walking around Apokeepsing, a city on an interstitial existential plane that was, and was not, identical to Poughkeepsie in some places, and not in others, was stranger and more confusing than if it had been a completely different place. We kept having the experience, over and over, of being completely comfortable and sure of where we were and then finding something unexpected and completely different. For example, imagine you are walking along a street you have walked along a hundred times—you know every house, every tree and bush. Then, you turn a corner you have turned a hundred times and there is a small volcano, with smoke and gasses issuing forth, and looking like it might erupt at any moment.

"Actually, the term for this is *fumarole,* although a small volcano is what it is," the Wolluf said. "Usually if there is one there are more, and often a big one, in the neighborhood, so we will watch our step."

We found ourselves on the road that would have

led to Spookhuizen and Chicken Nancy's house if we were in Poughkeepsie.

"I'd like to see if there's a Spookhuizen here," I said.

"Yes, good idea. Let's go," Molly said.

Then we met someone we knew! It was Jack! He was leading his horse.

"Jack!" Molly and I said.

Jack looked at us uncomprehendingly. It was obvious he didn't recognize us but assumed we knew him. He was friendly. "My mother told me to take this horse and trade it for something of value," he said.

It was also obvious that this Jack was a bit more simple-minded than the one we knew on the Pough-keepsie plane.

"Your name is Jack, right?" Molly asked.

"Close enough. It's Jake. I am going to the farmer to trade the horse."

"Your horse, Diablo? Don't you love him? Why would you want to trade him?"

"This horse is named Duivel, and he's just a horse. I'd rather have something valuable—besides, my mother told me to trade him. I don't know anything about a horse named Diablo. Would you like to come along?"

"We wouldn't miss it for the world," I said.

CHAPTER 47

Jake and the Bean Soup

We were on a road that corresponded to the road we knew in Poughkeepsie that led to the old stone barn, and Jake was heading in that direction.

"I'm really curious to see if there's a Spookhuizen here too," Molly said.

"So am I," I said.

It was to the old stone barn that Jake meant to go. It was a working farm in this version of reality. The farmer was big and fat, with a broad-brimmed hat, square-toed boots, a fringe of gray whiskers . . . and scales. He was like a human, and like a lizard. He was sitting on a bench in front of the old stone barn, sharpening a scythe.

Molly and I peered at the land behind the barn. There was no Spookhuizen—nothing but cultivated fields of beans or something.

"You want to swap for this horse?" Jake asked the farmer.

"It all depends, lad," the farmer said. "What did ye expect to get for horse?"

"Well, something of value, of course," Jake said. "Gold, for example."

"Eish! Not gold, that's certain," the farmer said. "He's not much, is horse. Not worth beans."

"I wouldn't trade him for beans," Jake said.

"Would thou trade horse for soup?" the farmer asked.

"Soup?"

"Aye, soup."

"What kind of soup?"

"Bean soup."

"I would not," Jake said.

"Not if it were magic bean soup?" the farmer asked.

"It's magic?"

"Aye, magic."

"Really magic?"

"This be the most magical bean soup ever was." The farmer reached into his overalls and pulled out a can. The label had a picture of a bean on it, and the lettering read *Farmer Grey's Magic Bean Soup. Kosher.* "It be kosher," he said.

"How many cans of this kosher magic bean soup would you trade for this fine horse?" Jake asked.

"One can for one horse," the farmer said.

"Only one?"

"It be magic," the farmer said.

Jake thought for a while. "Deal!" he said. He and the farmer spat on their palms and shook hands.

"By the way," Jake said to the farmer, "what kind of magic does this bean soup do?"

"What do I look like to you?" the farmer asked. "A magician? I'm a farmer. Ask me about crops or something, and I'll tell you. It's magic, and that's all I know about it. Now be on your way already—I have to go make with the scythe."

"Great trading," the Wolluf said.

"I know," Jake said.

CHAPTER 48

Like Mother, Like Son

What are you going to do with your magic bean soup?" I asked Jake.

"I will take it to my mother, of course," Jake said. "She will be pleased with me for making such a clever trade. Would you like to come along? Mommy will be happy to meet you."

"Oh, we are definitely coming along," Molly said. "I want to know how this story turns out."

The way to Jake's house was familiar. It was the same as the way to Chicken Nancy's house in the woods. Realizing where we were headed, we wondered if Chicken Nancy was Jake's mother in this semiplane. She was not. The woman who came out of the little house—which looked just like it did on the Poughkeepsie plane—was little and round, with a round head with her hair in a round bun on top, a round nose, and little round fingers on her little round hands. She had boots on, so we couldn't see if she had little round feet and little round toes, but it was a safe assumption.

"So! You're back from trading the horse already! What did you get for him? And hello, strangers. Welcome to our little home."

"I got this can of magic bean soup, Mommy," Jake said.

"What? You ninny! You fool! Come here and bend down so I can give you a slap on the noggin!"

Jake bent over, and his mother slapped him on the head. "You're a dolt! You traded a horse like that for a can of magic bean soup?"

"It was a good trade, Mommy!" Jake said. "My friends here said it was."

"I don't know who your friends are or where they came from," Jake's mother said. "But that horse was worth two cans of magic bean soup if he was worth a single bean! The farmer saw you coming, you nitwit!" She slapped him again.

"Mommy! You're embarrassing me in front of these people!" Jake shouted.

"Of course—where are my manners?" Jake's mommy said. "People I never saw before in my life, would you care to join us for some magic bean soup?"

"Only if you will share the cold fishcake sandwiches we brought with us," the Wolluf said.

"It will be a feast," Jake's mother said. "And I have leftover coffee from this morning."

"Yum," we all said.

The bean soup did not taste very magical. It did not even taste very beany. Jake's mother had to water it down so it would go around. It didn't seem to me that it would have been any better full strength. However, it was hot, and we were hungry. Not every meal has to be a banquet.

While we were munching and slurping, I noticed that I felt sort of giddy and woozy.

"I'm a little dizzy," Molly said.

"The room is wiggling," Jake said.

"This soup is laughing at me," Jake's mother said.

"I think we're high," the Wolluf said.

"Oh, look!" Jake's mother said. "It's our neighbor, Mr. Boonstengel!"

A small giant had entered the room. He looked exactly like Harold, our giant from back home in regular Poughkeepsie.

"Hello, everybody," the giant said.

"This will not mean anything to you, but you look exactly like a giant we know named Harold," I said.

"Well, it means hardly anything to me, but my name is Harold, and you do know me," Mr. Boonstengel said.

"You're our Harold?"

"I wouldn't say I was yours, but I know what you mean, and yes, I am the giant you took the boat ride with."

"How come you are here on this interstitial existential quasi plane?" I asked.

"I live here most of the time," Harold Boonstengel said. "I have a small Christmas tree farm just up the path. What have you been doing, eating magic bean soup? You all look sort of high."

"Yes. What is it with this stuff?" Molly asked.

"It makes you high—like Chef Chow's Hot and Spicy Oil," Boonstengel the giant said.

"Do people eat it because it makes them high?" I asked. "I find it sort of unpleasant."

"I don't know why people eat it," the giant said. "But it wears off pretty fast."

"Whoop!" Jake's mother shouted.

"Why did she whoop?" Molly asked me.

"Whoop!" I said. Something had poked my bottom, which surprised me, causing me to whoop.

"Whoop!" Molly said. "Something just poked my bottom. What goes on here?"

"It's my pet, Sparky," Harold said. "He's a golden gooser."

We looked down and saw an animal about the size of a large duck, and resembling a fireplug. It had a lustrous coat like a golden retriever.

"Sparky gooses people?"

"He's a golden gooser," Harold said.

"I am the Wolluf," the Wolluf said. "And if this creature gooses me, I will consider it a mark of disrespect."

"I think Sparky knows enough not to goose the Wolluf," Boonstengel said.

"Let us hope so," the Wolluf said. "Now I think we should depart."

"I was hoping you'd say that," Jake's mother said. "We have work to do around here and can't spend the day chatting with total strangers."

We thanked Jake and his mother for the unsatisfying and intoxicating magic bean soup, and left them, and Harold Boonstengel the giant, in the little house.

CHAPTER 49

Three Little Kids

Once the strangeness wears off, this mixed-up plane really isn't any more interesting than the regular Poughkeepsie one," Molly said.

"I agree," the Wolluf said. "Generally, one place is like another—it's what happens and what you observe that make the difference, wherever you are."

"And the idea of being here is because certain things can happen here, and be observed?" I asked.

"Perfectly right," the Wolluf said. "If I wanted to choose a plane of existence on the basis of having a pleasant excursion, I would have picked one with a lot of very good bakeries and restaurants."

"Are there such planes?" Molly asked.

"Certainly."

"Too bad this isn't one, specially if magic bean soup is any indication of the quality of the local cookery," I said.

We were just about to turn the corner onto the road that led back to the equivalent of downtown Poughkeepsie when three little kids appeared. They were all exactly the same height, wearing blue smocks, and barefooted. They had curly blond hair and faces like frogs.

"Attend us, strangers," the kids said in unison.

"Attend them," the Wolluf said. "This may be one of those things."

"You are in peril," the three little kids said all at once. I noticed the three little kids' feet were suspended two or three inches above the ground.

"What sort of peril?" the Wolluf asked.

"Beware!" the three little kids said. "Beware! Beware!"

"Is there something in particular we should beware of?" Molly asked.

"Beware the birdheads!" the three little kids said. "And keep with you the magic bag."

"Birdheads?"

"Magic bag?"

The three little kids produced a bag like a pillowcase. The bag was tied with cord.

"This bag is magic. Keep it with you always. It will lead you to your destiny."

"What is in the bag?"

"Never open the bag!" the three little kids said. "Never open the bag! Open the bag and you are doomed!" They handed us the bag. It contained something soft and moderately heavy.

"Do not lose the magic bag or leave it unattended in any way," the three little kids said, and then floated up into the treetops. "And beware the birdheads!" Then they were gone.

"We've got a magic bag," I said.

"Do we know what birdheads are?" Molly asked.

"Not a clue. What do you suppose is in the bag?"

"Let's open it and have a look."

"Think we'll be doomed if we do?"

"I don't believe in doomed. We'll just have a fast look."

"What do you think? Should we look?" I asked the Wolluf.

"I might," the Wolluf said. "But I am the Wolluf. I think the bag has to do with your destiny, not mine—so it's really up to you."

The three little kids appeared again, just over our heads. "Never open the bag!" they shouted in unison. "What's in that bag will spell your doom! Seriously!"

Then they were gone.

Then they were back again. "And remember about the birdheads too. Good luck."

Then they were gone.

We stood around for a while, waiting to see if they would come back. When it looked like they were done admonishing us, and not returning, we headed for downtown again.

CHAPTER 50

Birdheads

We found out what birdheads were. They were proctors, which was the name for cops in Apokeepsing. They wore black tailcoats and top hats, carried policemen's nightsticks, and of course had heads like birds, with beaks and feathers.

"Pull over, please," the first birdhead said.

"Pull over? We're walking. What do you mean, 'pull over'?"

"Just come to a stop, and answer our questions," the second birdhead said. "What's in the bag?"

"We don't know. It's supposed to be a magic bag. Some little kids gave it to us."

"Open the bag, please."

"We're not supposed to open it. It's a magic bag. The little kids said we'd be in trouble if we opened it."

"You'll be in trouble if you don't open it," the birdheads said.

"Better do what they say," the Wolluf said. "They are the law."

I undid the cord, opened the bag, and found myself looking into the eyes of Harold Boonstengel's pet.

"Where did you get the golden gooser?" the birdheads asked.

"As we told you, some little kids gave it to us. We didn't know it was the golden gooser in the bag."

"And you didn't steal it, I suppose?" one of the birdheads asked.

"No. Not stole. Never stole."

"And it comes as a complete surprise that one Harold Boonstengel, a local giant, reported his golden gooser missing not ten minutes ago?" the other birdhead asked.

"No. I mean, yes. I mean, we didn't know. We didn't take it."

"I told you not to do it," the Wolluf said. "I told you crime never pays."

"What?"

"Of course, we know you had nothing to do with

it, Mr. Wolluf," the birdheads said. "But the girl and the pussycat are under arrest."

"I'm a girl too," I said.

"The girl and the alleged girl, who is obviously a pussycat," the birdheads said. "We're taking you in."

"Clap the darbies on them," one of the birdheads said to the other, producing a pair of ugly-looking iron handcuffs.

"Are those the darbies?" I asked.

"There will be no need for those," the Wolluf said. "I guarantee they will come along quietly—and I will come with you myself."

"Well, seeing as how it's you that says it," the birdhead said. "We will accept your word, Mr. Wolluf, that these desperate criminal girls will not try anything funny while we march them off to gaol."

"By 'gaol' you mean jail?" Molly asked.

"That's where we take people who take things," the birdhead said.

CHAPTER 51

Marched

The birdhead proctors marched us through the streets to the gaol. A few citizens noticed us but didn't show any particular interest. One thing that interested me was seeing myself, or someone just about identical to me, coming the other way. I only saw her for a moment, before she turned a corner. The gaol was the building we knew as Susie's Chop Suey, a Chinese restaurant, on the Poughkeepsie plane. There they handed us over to the town gaoler, Moon Stoats. Moon Stoats was spectacularly ugly and evil-looking. He was short and fat and squat and brawny, with big bulging muscles and a face like an insane owl's.

"Wrongdoers!" Moon Stoats said. "If you try to escape or make noise, or just for no reason at all, I will torture you horribly, whip you, kick you, freeze you, fry you, squash you under a big stone, or pinch you without mercy. Here is your cell. You will await trial. I hope the court decides to hang you. I am also the town hangman, so I get extra for stringing you up." He locked Molly and me in, and went away, laughing like a maniac and rubbing his hands.

"He's unpleasant," Molly said.

"I have to agree," I said.

The Wolluf was not locked in. "I will go and find out what will happen to you. Do not worry about Moon Stoats—he's a monster and behaves like that with everyone. Don't think it is anything about you personally."

"What about just taking us off this miserable plane?" I asked the Wolluf. "Couldn't you do that?"

"What? You want to go home already?" the Wolluf asked.

"Well, yes! Anyway, before they hang us."

"Oh, I hardly think they hang people for stealing a golden gooser," the Wolluf said.

"Okay, before they whip us or pinch us, then. Besides, we did not steal the golden gooser."

"Hence they are going to give you a trial!" the Wolluf said. "Where you can prove your innocence. You don't want to leave before your trial."

"Of course not! What were we thinking?" I said. "Who would not want to stay in a cell in a jail run by a sadistic monster, and then be tried for a crime and probably subjected to some barbaric punishment?"

"Exactly!" the Wolluf said. "I will go now and see if I can arrange some kind of defense for you."

"I was being sarcastic," I said. But the Wolluf did not hear me. He was already at the end of the corridor, and by way of going out the door.

At the door, the Wolluf stopped, turned, and called to us, "Moon Stoats's daughter, Queenie, will be along later with something for you to eat. Bye!"

"Wait!" we shouted. "Get us out of here!" But the Wolluf was gone.

"He is not taking this seriously," I said.

"Which means that maybe it is not serious," Molly said.

"Or it means that the Wolluf is crazy, like so many people we meet," I said.

We looked around our cell. It was made of big, heavy, rough boards of wood, and the door was iron bars. There were two wooden benches, which we supposed were our beds. There was a bucket in the corner.

"Nice," Molly said.

"Deluxe," I said.

When it got to be night, Queenie showed up. She

did not look anything like Moon Stoats. She looked more or less like an idiot. She brought us some disgusting gruel.

"Here is some disgusting gruel," she said. She sounded more or less like an idiot.

"Are you cruel and horrible like your father?" Molly asked.

"No, I am nice. If it were up to me I would help you to escape. You should eat your gruel—you'll need your strength for the trial and ghastly punishments."

"Tell us about the trial," I said. "You can leave out the ghastly punishments."

"Basically, you're doomed," Queenie said. "Do you know who your judge will be?"

"Some judge?"

"Baas Kwaadwillig," Queenie said.

"Isn't he supposed to be bad?"

"He is a monster and a tyrant. He runs everything around here. My father admires him, if that tells you anything. You may be sure he will condemn you and sentence you to something horrible."

"But we're innocent. We didn't do anything."

"That makes no difference to Baas Kwaadwillig," Queenie said. "You know what you should do? You should assassinate him."

"What?"

"Do him in. Knock him off. Put an end to him. Bash him on the head with something heavy. Everyone will thank you for it."

"What are you talking about? You want us to kill somebody?"

"If you don't he will sentence you to an eternity in some icky pit. You don't want that, do you?"

"Not much, but we are not killing anybody."

"Just think it over. It's the right thing to do," Queenie said. "I have to go now. My father wants his disgusting gruel. I'll bring you a dagger or something just before the trial."

"When is the trial?"

"Midnight. You'll be in some terrible place by dawn. Your best chance is to kill Kwaadwillig." Queenie left.

"She's the weirdest one yet," Molly said.

"I wonder what's next," I said.

CHAPTER 52

Waiting for Midnight

Sitting in a dark cell gets one to thinking.

"You know, I really want to sort out this thing between Elizabeth Van Vreemdeling and myself," I said.

"You're still convinced that you are two different people?" Molly asked.

"I'm thinking that maybe I am Elizabeth, but not entirely. I mean, maybe part of me is her, but not all of me. It's more as though I have to find her so I can do something for her. I think it could be Elizabeth who's behind all the stuff that happens to us and not Chicken Nancy and the Wolluf making up a scenario and making us act it out."

"If I were already a wise woman like Chicken Nancy, I would just explain it to you," Molly said.

"*Already* a wise woman? Are you going to be one?"

"Yes, I think so. I think I will stay with Chicken Nancy and get her to teach me the wise woman trade."

"You already have talent for it," I said. "Knowing things, and reading minds and all. By the way, what is your opinion of our present situation? Are we really in trouble or not?"

"I think we are in for a few surprises," Molly said.

The three little kids turned up in our cell—which was almost a surprise.

"What did you do with the magic bag?" the three little kids said in unison. They were floating about midway between floor and ceiling.

"Why did you give us a magic bag with a stolen golden gooser in it?" I asked them.

"You opened the magic bag?" the three little kids said all together. "We told you not to open the magic bag!"

"Well, the birdheads made us open the magic bag, and now we are arrested and awaiting trial," Molly said.

"We told you if you opened the magic bag you'd get in trouble," the three little kids said.

"Who are you, anyway, you little nitwits?" Molly asked. "And what do we need to do to get you out of our lives?"

"We are your friends," the three annoying little kids said. "We are your only friends. You are in serious trouble, and you need your friends."

"The Wolluf is our friend," I said.

"The Wolluf left town," the three little kids said. "He went to see his auntie in Wappingers Falls."

Molly and I looked at each other. Could these little nuisances be telling the truth?

"We are angelic and spiritual beings who watch over you," the three little kids said. "We never lie."

Gloom.

"Take heart, weird girl and pussycat," the three little kids said.

"I'm a girl too," I said.

"We have gifts for you," the three little kids said. "To you, Molly, we give the elf fear gong. Strike it when something frightening happens. To you, pussycat-girl, we give a trouble fez. Wear it, because you are in trouble."

I put on the trouble fez, which was a kind of hat, and Molly hit the elf fear gong. The three little kids vanished.

"These things seem to work," Molly said.

CHAPTER 53

The Mystic Brothers of the Mystic Brotherhood

Queenie turned up. "They're coming," she said. "I couldn't find a dagger, but here's a big fork to kill Daas Kwaadwillig with."

"Get away from us, maniac," I said.

Molly hit the elf fear gong.

A bunch of men appeared in the corridor outside our cell. With them was Moon Stoats, jingling his keys. The men were all wearing golden robes and pussycat masks.

"Unlock the cell, gaoler," one of the men said. "It is time to take them to the Mystic Temple."

"They're to be hanged, aren't they?" Moon Stoats asked eagerly.

"Unlock the cell."

CHAPTER 54

In the Mystic Temple

The guys in the pussycat masks led us out of the gaol. Under the streetlights there was a crowd waiting, and a band wearing top hats and led by a man with an open umbrella. The head pussycat-mask guy gave a signal to the open-umbrella guy, the open-umbrella guy raised his umbrella, and the musicians raised their horns and clarinets and saxophones and began playing a hot number.

With the band before us, bouncing and strutting, the leader waving his umbrella, and the crowd cheering, we started off with pussycat-mask men on all sides of us. It was a good band, and Molly and I couldn't help but march along with a bounce in our step. The pussycat-mask men were waving to the crowd, and pretty soon we were doing it too. For a second I saw the girl who looked exactly like me, and then I lost sight of her. The guys in the band were swinging and weaving, dancing and turning, and we could see the umbrella bobbing up and down. Molly and I tried some fancy stepping, and the people in the crowd whistled and shouted.

It was a parade, a swinging parade. We swung around the corner and up another street, then up the steps and through the doors of the Temple of the Mystic Brotherhood.

The head pussycat-mask man said to us, "You are in the Mystic Temple. Behave nicely. I will take you to your seats in the Great Hall. There you will wait quietly. Baas Kwaadwillig will be here soon."

"We heard he was as bad as could be," I said.

"No, he is as good as can be," the Mystic Brother said. "Our order is devoted to justice and harmony, and he is our leader. If you are girls of goodwill and courage, no harm will come to you and you will receive the blessings of enlightenment."

"Is that a fact?" Molly asked.

"It is a fact," the pussycat-face said. "All will become clear, and you will understand everything."

"That will be a nice change," Molly said.

The seats he conducted us to were in a large room, like an auditorium, which I recognized as the inside of the Panopticon Theatre, which the Wolluf had told us it would later become.

"Speaking of the Wolluf," Molly said, reading my mind, "can you believe he took off and left us here on our own so he could visit his auntie?"

"I can't believe he has an auntie," I said.

There was a stage at the front of the auditorium, and behind it, where the screen would be, was a gigantic painting, a mural. I found it very interesting. There were some familiar things in it—Spookhuizen, for example, and the beech trees around it, and one very big beech tree, bigger than all the others. And there were flying fuzzballs, like the ones we had seen. Some of the fuzzballs looked like the fuzzballs I remembered, and some of them had cat faces in them, some had whole cats in them, and some of them *were* cats. There were also cats all around the painting, some of them drinking from saucers of milk. And that was everything in the mural—except a picture of me! I was standing next to the extra-large beech tree.

"Do you see that?" I asked Molly.

"Sure do."

"Do you understand it?"

"Almost."

"I don't think we're here to be tried for stealing a golden gooser," I said.

"Neither do I," Molly said.

CHAPTER 55

De Boom Is De Sleutel

The Mystic Brothers filed in to the auditorium and sat down all around us. They were more or less human, most of them. They had taken off their pussycat masks and were now wearing hats that looked like pineapples, and carrying sprigs of catnip. I recognized the voice of the one who had been the head pussycat-mask man. He stood on the stage, raised his arms, and said, "De boom is de sleutel!"

All the Mystic Brothers in the seats raised their arms and said, "De boom is de sleutel!"

"What does that mean?" I whispered to Molly.

"It's Dwergish, or something close to Dwergish," Molly said. "I think it means, 'the tree is the key.'"

"Be silent!" the guy on the stage said. "Let us

enter a state of contemplative calm. Let our minds be still. Let us close our eyes and put our hands on our knees, in the ancient posture taught to our first master by the priests of Egypt. Compose yourselves, Brothers of the Mystic Temple. The master comes!"

The Mystic Brothers put their hands on their knees and sat very quietly with their eyes closed. We sat quietly too, but we did not close our eyes. We saw the head pussycat-mask man leave the stage, and after a while Baas Kwaadwillig appeared. He had a fancier gold robe, and a bigger pineapple hat than the others. He looked as scary as the time we saw him in the street, but not as evil.

"De boom is de sleutel!" he said with arms raised, and the brothers raised their arms and responded, "De boom is de sleutel!"

"Mystic Brothers!" Baas Kwaadwillig said. "Our order is as old as the tree in Eden, as old as Yggdrasil, the tree of the world, as old as the Grizzly Giant in the redwood forest of California, as old as the Bristlecone Pine. For thousands of years we have stood for understanding and goodness, and the keeping of great secrets. Time and again we have preserved wisdom in dark times when the forces of evil have attempted to extinguish the light and to extirpate our teachings, root and branch."

"I get it," Molly whispered to me. "They're tree worshipers."

"Silence!" Baas Kwaadwillig boomed. "Tonight is a singular night in our history, for we have new candidates for membership in the order—and for the first time one of the initiates is a little girl and the other is a pussycat."

"I'm a girl too," I said.

"A little girl and another girl who is similar to a pussycat," Baas Kwaadwillig said. "Let the candidates come forward!"

"He means us," I whispered to Molly.

The Mystic Brothers sitting beside us stood up so we could make our way across the row of seats to the aisle.

"Well, let's go forward," Molly said. We went forward and stood before the stage.

"If you succeed in your initiation, you will be the first female Brothers of the Mystic Temple," Baas Kwaadwillig said. "And I suppose that would make you Sisters of the Mystic Temple. Of course, if you fail your initiation, you will die. Do you accept this?"

"Do we have a choice?" I asked.

"No."

"Then we accept," I said.

"Can you promise to be kind to animals, to change

your socks and underwear every day, or as often as is practicable, and to never eat cold beet borscht with sour cream, except in the case of starvation? Think well before you answer, for these promises are inviolable."

"You have a problem with any of those?" Molly whispered to me.

"None," I whispered.

"We promise," we both said.

"De boom is de sleutel," Baas Kwaadwillig said. "We now entrust you with the Sacred Snooker Stick, made of ancient wood. Guard it well." He handed us a long, skinny piece of wood resembling a pool cue. The Mystic Brothers applauded.

"Is that it? Are we initiated?" Molly asked.

"Not yet," Baas Kwaadwillig said. "First you must undergo the trials."

"Oh yes, the trial," I said. "About the golden gooser. Well, we can explain—"

"Silence!" Baas Kwaadwillig bellowed. "This has nothing to do with a golden gooser. You must undergo two dangerous and frightening trials—the Trial of Hot, and the Trial of Wet. Only if you survive them will you be members of our order. Naturally, if you do not survive them . . ."

"Death," Molly and I said.

"Death," Baas Kwaadwillig said.

CHAPTER 56

Sub-sub-sub-sub-sub

Two of the Mystic Brothers conducted us up the little flight of stairs at the side of the stage. It turned out there was a door in the mural, right in the middle of the very big tree. The two brothers and Baas Kwaadwillig pushed us through and followed us. We were in a little room hung with ropes, and there was a big basket in the middle.

"The trials will take place in the sub-sub-sub-sub-sub-basement, beneath the temple," Baas Kwaadwillig said. "They are very scary trials, and once you have begun them no one can help you. Do you understand this?"

We said we did.

"I see you have the elf fear gong, and a trouble fez," Baas Kwaadwillig said. "And you have the Sacred Snooker Stick. These objects will protect you if your hearts are pure. Are you ready to begin your trials?"

We said we were.

"Step into the basket."

We stepped into the basket. It was quite large enough for both of us.

"They are in the basket," the two brothers said.

"Lower away," Baas Kwaadwillig said.

We felt something slide underneath us. It was a trapdoor opening. The basket rocked a little, and we began to sink into darkness. The last thing we saw was the brothers paying out rope. They were lowering us.

We automatically sat down to steady the basket. The dim light that came from the open trapdoor soon faded, and looking upward we could see the trapdoor as a gray square getting smaller and dimmer—and then we were in darkness. This darkness was of the blackest black, and then it got blacker. It was impossible to tell how fast we were descending, or even that we were moving at all. I couldn't remember ever seeing it so dark.

"I don't suppose you have a match," I asked Molly.

"All I have is this elf fear gong," Molly said. "And I'm getting ready to ring it."

It was impossible to tell how far we had been lowered, or how fast we were going, or even how much time had passed. At one point I reached out to see if I could feel a wall or anything, but all I could feel was nothing. And all I could hear was silence.

For some reason, I kept thinking about the girl who looked exactly like me, the one I had seen in the street while we were being taken here and there. Also for no reason I knew of, I thought it was important that I had seen her. I was going to mention it to Molly, but she spoke first.

"The Trial of Hot, and the Trial of Wet," she said. "Would that be fire and water, do you think?"

"So, what are you thinking? We're going to be burned and drowned?"

"Well, something like that. Anyway, that's what it sounds like."

"Remind me why we agreed to this."

"Because he said if we didn't it would mean death."

"Oh, yes—that."

CHAPTER 57

Thump

The basket hit bottom with a thump. It was every bit as dark as it had been on the way down. We just sat there for a while, not speaking.

When we did speak, there was an echo. I could feel that we were in an enormous open space—I sensed it was much bigger than the whole Mystic Temple. Except for our voices, and the echo, it was completely silent.

"We're in a mine or something," I said.

"How are we going to get out of here?" Molly asked.

"You don't think they lowered us down here and are just going to leave us to die, do you?" I asked.

"Or, has it occurred to you that these Mystic Brothers are crazy as bats?" Molly asked. "Maybe they lower people down here expecting them to go through some goofy trials, and when they never see them again they assume they failed, or they just forget about them. I mean, these are grown adults who wear pussycat masks and pineapples on their heads."

"And we let them lower us into some kind of gigantic pit," I said. "We are the crazy ones."

"Shall we holler?" Molly asked.

"Yes. Let's do that," I said.

We started to holler, but the echo got so loud, it made us dizzy and scared us.

"Let's not holler," I said.

"What do you suggest?" Molly asked.

"Well, we can get out of the basket. And start feeling our way around."

We got out of the basket. The floor of the place we were in was covered with gravel and loose stones. When stepped on, it made an unpleasant high-pitched squeaking sound—except in some spots where the stones made a nice mellow sound like a woodblock being hit with a drumstick or castanets.

"Oh! I just thought of something," Molly said. "What if there are pits?"

"Pits?"

"Pits. In all this blackness, we could easily fall

into a deep pit and break our necks. How do we know there aren't pits?"

"Good point," I said. "We could just stay right here by the basket and wait for them to pull it up."

"I think we just did that," Molly said.

"What do you mean?" I said, and then, "Oh! It's gone! Do you think they pulled it up?"

"Presumably."

"And they would be able to tell by the weight that we weren't in it."

"Right."

"So they had no intention of pulling us back up. What's that noise?"

"That's me hitting the elf fear gong," Molly said.

"Well, stop for a minute, and let's think," I said. "What's the best thing to do?"

"Find our way out of here and not fall into any pits," Molly said. "You have a trouble fez. Put it on and see if anything occurs to you."

"Have you noticed that in some spots the floor makes an annoying squeaky sound and in others it makes a nice mellow clicking?" I asked Molly.

"I did notice that," Molly said.

"I am noticing that the mellow-clicking spots are grouped together, and contiguous," I said. "What happens if we step only on those?"

Molly experimented. "I think they are laid out in a line," she said. "It's like a path or a road."

"Maybe that is so we can follow in a direction even though it's completely dark," I said.

"So we . . ."

"Follow the mellow click road!"

"Follow the mellow click road!"

CHAPTER 58

Following

We made our way along, listening for the mellow clicks, stepping carefully lest we fall into a pit. I tried to be cheerful, but I couldn't manage it. It was depressing, and dark, and scary, and lonely.

"You know what?" Molly asked me.

"What?"

"I miss my mommy and daddy."

"You know what?" I asked Molly.

"What?"

"I miss my mommy and daddy too."

"I thought you didn't remember your mommy and daddy."

"I don't. That's the odd part. I think I am missing Elizabeth Van Vreemdeling's mommy and daddy."

"That is odd."

"I know. I think I am sort of working out the Elizabeth thing. I think maybe I am she, and also me. As to that other girl I saw who looked just like us—I mean her and me—I'm starting to have an idea."

The three little kids appeared, floating over our heads as usual. They each had a candle. "Take heart, brave girl, and brave pussycat companion," the three little kids said.

"I am a girl too," I said.

"Take heart! Take heart! Your journey nears its end! If you are brave you will be rewarded, and all will be well!"

"So can you tell us if we are going in the right direction?"

"For if you are of pure heart, and have courage, you will overcome even the greatest dangers!"

"Is there a way out of here?"

"So be brave, girl and pussycat, and you shall prevail. And now, farewell. Your destiny awaits you!"

"Could you leave those candles with us?"

And the three little kids were gone.

"You know, I kind of hate them," I said.

"So do I," Molly said.

It seemed even darker once the three little kids had left with their candles. Of course, they had been above us, and we had been looking up at them. Had it occurred to us to look around, we might have gotten an idea of where we were in the candlelight, but they had come and gone so quickly, we never had a chance to think of that.

Then we heard a voice. It seemed to come from all directions. "It is time! Prepare yourselves for the first ordeal. Prepare yourselves for the Trial of Hot!"

Prepare? Prepare how? On one hand, it felt sort of good that the Mystic Brothers had not forgotten about us and we were not completely alone. On the other hand, we were supposed to be preparing for the Trial of Hot, and we had no idea how to do that.

"If there's fire involved, that means there will be light too," I said. "Then at least we can get some idea of what's around us, and maybe even see a way out."

Something small and light bounced off my head. "What's that? A bat?"

Another one hit me.

"There are things hitting me!" I said.

"Me too!" Molly said. "We're being pelted with . . ."

I caught ahold of one of the things and felt it. It was smooth, and tapered, and had a stem. "This feels like a Mexican pepper!" I said.

"We're being pelted with jalapeños!" Molly said.

"Peppers? That's the Trial of Hot?"

I could hear wheezing and snorting and giggling in the darkness. It was obvious, the Mystic Brothers had gathered in the pit, or mine, or basement, or whatever it was, and were throwing little hot peppers at us.

"The Trial of Hot! You have survived! You live!" the voice that came from everywhere said. "Continue on your quest, worthy girl and worthy pussycat!"

"I'm a girl too!" I shouted.

"Oh, for pity's sake," Molly said. "Hot peppers! What's next? Squirt guns?"

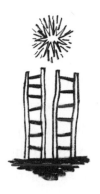

CHAPTER 59

A Light!

Far away we saw a tiny twinkling light! It looked like a distant star.

"Look!" Molly said.

"I'm looking!" I said.

"Run!" Molly said.

"I'm running!" I said.

We were excited. The light looked friendly. It seemed brighter as we ran toward it. It was a lantern, or a candle—we didn't know what it was, but we felt it was our best friend.

"The Trial of Wet!" the voice from everywhere shouted, and we were squirted with water from all sides. This time the Mystic Brothers were giggling out loud.

Squirt, squirt, squirt, squirt. We were drenched.

"What idiots!" Molly said.

"Really," I said.

The squirting stopped.

"Once again, you have survived!" the voice said. "You are accepted into the Mystic Brotherhood. You may purchase robes, pussycat masks—only necessary for one of you—and sacred pineapple headdresses. Congratulations! You may depart the sacred chamber."

Then we were alone again. There was no sound of anyone else. We approached the light, which turned out to be a fat candle on a rock.

We stood there, wet.

"What do you think?" Molly asked. "We are in the ordinary basement of the temple, and the nitwits just lowered us very slowly?"

"Something like that," I said. "Let's take the candle and find the way out of here."

"I am never joining anything after this," Molly said. "Especially anything secret."

"That goes double for me," I said.

We found a couple of ladders that went up into the darkness. Painted on the wall with whitewash next to one ladder was a sign that read ORDINARY LADDER, and next to the other ladder was one that read MYSTIC LADDER.

"Guess what," I said. "I'm for using the ordinary ladder. If we go up the other one they will probably dump buckets on us, or set off firecrackers, or try to make us buy pineapple hats."

"I agree," Molly said. "Let's start climbing. I bet it's only ten feet."

"I bet it's eight feet."

CHAPTER 60

Much More

It was more like a hundred feet. I have plenty of experience as a mountain climber, and Molly as a dwerg can climb right up a smooth wall, but it was still a long, hard climb. The ladder was dirty and dusty, and went up a narrow wooden shaft. We figured we had been lowered into a mine after all.

"I hate those Mystic Brothers," Molly said.

"Oh, I hate them too," I said.

"Why are you climbing with the Sacred Snooker Stick?" Molly asked me. "Doesn't it make it harder for you?"

"It's mine," I said. "They gave it to me."

"They gave it to both of us," Molly said. "But you may have my share."

"I am not going down in the earth and stumbling around in the dark and having Mexican peppers thrown at me and getting squirted and not even get a Sacred Snooker Stick out of it," I said. "Thanks for your share. I need this Snooker Stick." I had no idea why I said that or what I needed it for.

"De boom is de sleutel," Molly said.

CHAPTER 61

Finally!

We got to the top of the ladder and clambered through a little door in a wall to find we were looking at a really big flying saucer! It was huge, and glowing— sitting on the ground in what looked like a park, with an enormous metal man standing in front of it. He was glowing too, and he was close to us, just a few feet away! Our mouths dropped open. We were too surprised and scared to move.

Then we heard a very loud voice—it was a woman's voice—saying, "Klaatu barada nikto." I felt chills down my spine. I felt amazement and awe. I felt . . . recognition.

"Wait a second," I said.

"Yeah, I saw this movie too," Molly said.

"Do you realize where we are?" I asked.

"We're on the back side of a movie screen," Molly said. "The movie is being projected on the other side. It's *The Day the Earth Stood Still*. It's been playing at the Panopticon in Poughkeepsie."

"Which would make sense, because this *is* the Panopticon in Poughkeepsie," I said.

"You think?" Molly asked.

"It's easily tested," I said. "Let's go through that side door with the red Exit sign over it."

We went though the door and found ourselves in the alley next to the movie house. We walked to the street, and there was good old Poughkeepsie as we knew it. And as if to prove we were back in our old time and space, who should come walking along, carrying a gallon jar of beet borscht from Adams's Farm Market, but Professor Tag!

"Professor Tag!" we shouted.

"Hello, girls," the professor said. "What have you been up to? Would you like to come to my house to enjoy some borscht?"

"We swore an oath not to," Molly said. "But we have a lot to tell you. Would you come with us to Chicken Nancy's house?"

"Of course," Professor Tag said. "I'll just take the borscht along as a present for the old lady. That's a nice Sacred Snooker Stick—where did you get it?"

"We'll tell you everything when we get to Chicken Nancy's."

CHAPTER 62

Tell Everything!

I checked my reflection in store windows as we passed. I had lost the enhanced pussycatness that had happened while we were on the semi-Poughkeepsie plane. This caused mixed feelings—I was happy to see the more familiar me, but I thought I had looked better with fur all over.

When we got to Chicken Nancy's little house in the woods she was outside, mixing sugar and yeast into a big tub of cornmeal mush.

"I brought you borscht," Professor Tag said.

"Pour it right in here," Chicken Nancy said. "It will give it age. Hello, girls. Did you learn things on your trip with the Wolluf?"

"We certainly did, and we have questions to ask you," Molly said. "For instance, is it true that you and the Wolluf are secretly Audrey's parents? Are you a leprechaun? Is there a pot of gold buried under the floor of your little house? Do you come from Venus? Am I actually a princess from a magical realm? Has all this been a dream?"

"No," Chicken Nancy said. "Why do you ask?"

"I just wanted to have something to say," Molly said. "Once Audrey gets started, she's going to do all the talking."

"Understood," Chicken Nancy said.

"Oh, there is one thing," Molly said. "I was thinking I would just live here with you for a few years and learn to be a wise woman. Is that okay?"

"I assumed we had already agreed about that," Chicken Nancy said.

"Cool," Molly said. "I just wanted to make it official. I'll be quiet now. Audrey, you go."

Of course, I had to bring Chicken Nancy and Professor Tag up to date, telling them about all the things that had happened since we went underground with the Wolluf. "By the way, what was with the Wolluf running out on us like that?" I asked Chicken Nancy.

"He's the Wolluf," Chicken Nancy said. "He's wild and unpredictable—but you must admit, no harm came to you. I think you have to give him credit for knowing that was how it would be. But what I am waiting to hear is whether you learned anything or figured anything out."

"I was coming to that," I said. "It's all about Elizabeth Van Vreemdeling. First you show me a picture of her, and it looks just like me. Molly thinks I actually am Elizabeth Van Vreemdeling. You say maybe I am. Professor Tag says I definitely am—"

"I do say that," the professor said.

"The trolls on Bannerman's Island think I am, and so it goes. After a while, I started thinking I am . . . only I know I'm not . . . only I have the feeling I am. It gets all confusing. And then I started feeling that I am and I am not. I am me, Audrey, and I am Elizabeth Van Vreemdeling too, and also a girl I saw in a crowd on the semi-Poughkeepsie plane."

"Are you saying you are one of those multiple personalities?" Professor Tag asked. "I was just reading about those—people who have several different imaginary persons within them."

"I am saying I am a multiple person—not just personality," I said. "I don't have it all worked out. Maybe it's that there is one of us, or of me, on this plane—that would be Elizabeth—and one on the plane I came from—that would be me—and one on the quasi-Poughkeepsian plane Molly and I just visited—that would be the girl I saw. And there's the time thing—that's confusing. Maybe there has been a whole string of Elizabeths, or Audreys, over time.

"But here's the thing I am sure of—I have to do something for Elizabeth. Maybe the whole reason I came to Poughkeepsie was to do this thing for her."

"And do you know what that thing is?" Chicken Nancy asked.

"Not exactly. I almost know it. It's right on the tip of my brain, so to speak. What I do know is that it has something to do with the flying pussycats."

Molly was grinning. So was Chicken Nancy.

"Flying pussycats?" Professor Tag asked.

"They're not flying saucers. They're not spaceships like in the movies. They're not machines. They're alive, and if they're not pussycats, they're something pretty close to pussycats."

"What are you saying? That there are pussycats capable of interplanetary travel?" the professor asked.

"What day is this?" I asked.

"Wednesday," Professor Tag said.

"Come with me to Spookhuizen tonight, and I'll show you," I said.

CHAPTER 63

Plans

I'll come along," Chicken Nancy said. "Not only is it Wednesday, but this is the day of the year when a great ball would be held at Spookhuizen. I used to attend those balls. It will be pleasant to visit on this night, and remember them. In fact, let's dress up fancy tonight."

"Dress up fancy?" Molly asked.

"Yes! Call it an old woman's whim," Chicken Nancy said. "I have a couple of ball gowns you girls would look lovely in."

"I can go home and put on my kilt and regalia!" Professor Tag said.

"You have a kilt and regalia?"

"Oh, yes. The Royal Scottish Accountants—I am a member."

"It will be fun," Chicken Nancy said. "Do you agree?"

"I'll bet one of the gowns belonged to Elizabeth Van Vreemdeling," Molly said.

"As a matter of fact . . ." Chicken Nancy said.

"We can fix up our hair too," I said.

"Take naps!" Chicken Nancy said. "Then we'll dress, and have an elegant meal, and all go to Spookhuizen, just as though we were going to a ball in the old times."

CHAPTER 64

I Know What I Know

Before we took our naps, which we needed after being initiated all night long, Molly asked me, "What do you plan to show us at Spookhuizen tonight?"

"It's going to come to me," I said. "I'm going to have an idea, and something will happen. It will all be made clear."

"And how do you know all this?" Molly asked.

"I just know it," I said.

"Well, you're practically getting to be a dwerg for knowing things," Molly said.

"I learned from the best," I said.

And we both fell asleep.

CHAPTER 65

Razzle-Dazzle

The ball gowns from Chicken Nancy's closet must have come from the same time as the cloaks. They were gowns for children or young people, simple and graceful. Mine was blue and Molly's was green. They were soft and light, with long flowing skirts that made us look as though we were gliding when we walked. I felt good wearing mine.

Chicken Nancy's gown was a different sort of thing entirely. It was dark green and had gold fringes, and tassels, and Chicken Nancy had a tall feather thing on top of her head and carried a little sparkly bag she said was a reticule. She had piled her hair on top of her head too, making her look quite tall, and had gloves that came up to the elbow.

"I wore this once at a party attended by Mr. Lincoln," Chicken Nancy said.

Professor Tag showed up wearing the full regalia of the Royal Scottish Accountants. This consisted of a big kilt, a jacket with silver buttons, a ruffled shirt, shoes with silver buckles, a sort of plaid blanket over his shoulder, and a bonnet with a feather, also various buckles, ribbons, hunks of animal fur, leather, daggers, knives, and fountain pens tucked into his socks and cuffs, strapped around his waist, and variously attached to his costume.

"You ladies all look beautiful," the professor said. "And as you see, I too look beautiful. Now let us go out on the razzle-dazzle. It will be my honor to escort you to a fine dining establishment favored by the aristocracy."

We went to Angelina's Pizza and Pasta.

"I've always wanted to come here," Molly said.

"It's the eggplant festival," Professor Tag said.

"A six-course meal, every dish a celebration of the melanzana or aubergine, known to you as the noble eggplant, and each course served on a fresh paper plate," the proprietor said. He was a little bald guy with a mustache. "I will start you off with an individual miniature eggplant pizza."

"What is the second course?" Professor Tag asked.

"A full-size eggplant pizza, followed by spaghetti with eggplant bits, then eggplant parmigiana, the sautéed eggplant medley, and eggplant chips."

"Do you have eggplant sauce for the chips?" I asked.

"It's my grandmother's recipe."

"It all sounds so delicious," Chicken Nancy said.

"Please select cold beverages from the cooler," the little guy said. "Your waitress will bring you straws, and plastic knives and forks."

"This place had a very good write-up in the *Poughkeepsie Journal*," Professor Tag said. "We were lucky to get a reservation."

It was fun being all dressed up and dining in a fine restaurant. Our conversation was refined and entertaining. Professor Tag told the story about the dancing doll that did not work, which he told very well, and we enjoyed it even though we had heard it before. Molly told us jokes the dwergs like to tell. This is an example of a dwergish joke:

Dwerg (standing on the east bank of a river, and calling to a dwerg on the west bank of the river): Hey, dwerg! How do I get to the other side?

Other dwerg (standing on the west bank of the river): Silly dwerg! You're already on the other side!

We laughed politely.

Chicken Nancy told us many facts about the eggplant, or *solanum melongena* (*melongena* being its ancient name in Sanskrit). It is the only member of the deadly nightshade family to have originated in the Eastern Hemisphere, and it is related to the tomato. In Europe it was believed to cause insanity and was known as the "mad apple." Thomas Jefferson introduced it to North America.

I did not talk about what I planned to demonstrate at Spookhuizen when it got dark, because I didn't precisely know what I was going to do—but I knew I would know when the time came.

CHAPTER 66

The Time Has Come

The sun was getting low as we finished our dessert, which had no eggplant—it was individual mini-cheesecakes that came wrapped in cellophane, and paper cups of delicious coffee.

"Let us be on our way," Professor Tag said. We said goodbye to John, the pizza and pasta proprietor, and went out into the street, wearing our party clothes, and me carrying my Sacred Snooker Stick.

Everything was normal at the old stone barn. We saw the fritter lady through the window, bustling around her shop as usual, but instead of the usual apron, sticky with apple goo, she was wearing a nice gigantic orange dress.

"Even Clarinda Quackenboss is dressed up tonight," Chicken Nancy said.

We passed through the barn and onto the grounds of Spookhuizen. The tops of the beech trees were glowing golden in the last rays of the sun, and the old house was its ghostly self in the distance. The lawns looked freshly mowed, and there was a good cut-grass smell.

We strolled among the trees, feeling fine after our dinner and cutting a stylish figure in our fancy clothes. It was all very civilized and pleasant.

"I have a feeling the flying saucers . . . uh, flying pussycats . . . will be putting on a particularly good show," Professor Tag said.

"Depend on it," Chicken Nancy said. "This is just like so many nights I remember from when I was a girl no older than these two."

"Back in the old times, you said, Elizabeth Van Vreemdeling disappeared," Molly said. "How did she come to disappear, and what or who made her do that?"

"Can't you guess?" Chicken Nancy said.

"I can guess, but I thought instead I would just ask you," Molly said.

"Well, as Audrey here seems to have worked out, Elizabeth was quite an important person in certain ways," Chicken Nancy said. "And she was good, as opposed to bad. So someone quite bad disappeared her."

"And who would that have been?" Molly asked.

"Who do you think it was, Audrey?" Chicken Nancy asked me.

"Was it Matthias Krenzer, the old Dutch censor who stole the censer from the Old Dutch Church and was demoted to an old Dutch cleanser, and later opened a muffinery and became the Muffin Man, and is completely evil, and once menaced Molly and me, until Molly instinctively summoned the vicious Christmas tree spirits to chase him away?" I guessed.

"Maybe," Chicken Nancy said. "Look! It's nearly dark!"

I smelled something like pineapple and mint.

CHAPTER 67

The Best Ever

This time the fuzzballs didn't appear a long way off and then come closer. This time they were right above our heads, all at once, and there were lots of them! They moved around among us, almost touching us. I could feel their warmth, and something else—it was like happiness, or love. And I could hear the sound they made—they were purring!

Up to now, I had sort of half known things, suspected them, had vague ideas and hunches. I knew I was getting closer to understanding something, but it was as though I could only see what I was getting at by glancing out of the corners of my eye—if I looked directly at it, it would elude me, be invisible. Now, suddenly, I understood everything. I couldn't have put it in words—it didn't have words—but I knew what I had to do.

I raised the Sacred Snooker Stick, held it up as high as I could, and stood on tiptoe. Instantly, the flying fuzzballs, the space-pussycat things, extended their light and touched the Sacred Snooker Stick with electricity, or space-pussycat lightning, or liquid fire, or . . . I didn't know what it was, but it was powerful stuff. It ran down the Sacred Snooker Stick, lighting it up, and down my arm, and all around me—it got into my brain. And I felt my brain light up! Then I *really* knew everything. I don't mean just everything about me, and who I was and what I was supposed to do, and Elizabeth Van Vreemdeling, and the pussycats—I mean I knew everything about everything. And that was more than my brain could deal with, so it just sort of switched itself off. Part of me was still me, the me I usually was and always had been—that part was watching me. I saw myself walk up to the very biggest, most gnarled and twisted amazing old beech tree on the place and give it an enormous whack on the trunk with the Sacred Snooker Stick.

The whole tree shuddered and shook. It wiggled its branches. Leaves fluttered down. Sparks and flashes of light ran up and down the trunk. Then the mighty trunk split open and out stepped . . .

Me!

Of course, it wasn't me. I mean, it wasn't *just* me—it was her too. It was Elizabeth Van Vreemdeling! There I was, me, the me I had been all along, being watched by the part of me that had stepped outside of me when the pussycat-lightning hit me—and that me was partly Elizabeth, and was facing Elizabeth, who was partly me. I should have been a lot more confused than I was, but it actually all felt sort of normal in a completely abnormal way.

"Nice to see you," the me that was mostly Elizabeth said to the me that was mostly me. "I got sick of being stuck inside that tree at least a hundred years ago."

"Um. Glad I could be of service," I said.

She was even wearing the same sort of gown as the one I had on.

"You don't have an experience like this every day, do you?" Me/Elizabeth said.

"No, I can honestly say this is a first," I said to my other self.

"I expect we'll get sorted out and separate into two people by and by," Elizabeth said.

I was becoming aware that the two of us were alone on the avenue of beech trees. Molly, Chicken Nancy, Professor Tag, and the flying fuzzball space-pussycats all had disappeared. I also noticed that the windows of Spookhuizen were glittering with light and the doors were open, and I could hear music playing.

"The ball," Elizabeth said.

"The ball?"

"The ball. There's a ball going on. You're dressed for it, so you must have known. Shall we go in?"

CHAPTER 68

The Ball at Spookhuizen

Almost everybody was a cat, more or less, or to some extent. Some were no different from regular pussycats one sees every day. Others were larger, ranging to almost the size of lions, and still others appeared to be partly or mostly human, or humanlike. Still others seemed to be a combination of cat and species I didn't recognize, and some were humans with a cat feature or two, like me. Like Elizabeth. Those who wore clothes were wearing fancy ones. There was a pussycat orchestra, lots of candles in crystal chandeliers, a long table with lots of cakes and desserts, and a fountain of some kind of wine or punch. There were also some humans, and others.

When Elizabeth and I came in, everyone turned toward us and applauded—it was a soft sort of applause, clapping paws together—and smiled and nodded to us.

"That's for you," Elizabeth said. "For finding me, and getting me out of the tree."

Apparently, Elizabeth was important—some kind of ambassador, or maybe a beacon for the space cats, or she was royalty or something. Anyway, they were all glad she had gotten loose from the tree, and they were all happy about me being the one who did it. Lots of cats, cat-people, and people, and things came up and talked to us, and brought me ice cream, and patted my head, and purred at me. It was a little embarrassing, and confusing—so many little conversations one after another, and sometimes two or three at once. I was able to pick up that the idea that Elizabeth and I were different editions of the same person, each belonging to a particular place and plane, was about right. She belonged to this one, the girl I had seen on the in-between Poughkeepsie plane belonged there, and I belonged to the one I came from.

I saw Chicken Nancy talking to some cats, and Professor Tag was dancing with one. Molly was with some dwergs—they appeared to be telling jokes and laughing. The Hudson River trolls were in a little room off the main room, playing cards. Harold the giant was there, and Alexandra Van Dood, and the Gleybners!

"Audrey dear!" Mrs. Gleybner said to me. "Isn't this a nice party? I think some of the guests may be extraterrestrials."

"The Wolluf is outside in the bushes," Elizabeth told me in answer to a question that had just occurred to me—not so much reading my mind as having one exactly like it. "He enjoys social occasions but doesn't want to come in and terrify and disgust everyone." So I knew he had gone back to his usual unbearable appearance. I thought Molly or I should take him some ice cream or a piece of cake.

I felt completely comfortable with Elizabeth, naturally, since we were the same person, but it also felt slightly weird to be with her. I was literally beside myself. We didn't speak much, not needing to. We both knew that we would have to sort ourselves out sooner or later. It would not do for both of us to stay in the same time and space. But there was no rush about it, we both thought. We'd get around to it. I was really here as a tourist, and presumably would be going back to from whence I had come, or someplace else, but not just yet.

CHAPTER 69

The Grand Dance

Everyone take your places for the grand dance!"
someone shouted.

All of a sudden, I felt like dancing. I had never
danced much, but now I wanted to. Everyone else
apparently felt the same way, because they all began
a very complicated dance that involved all the guests.
This was no ordinary dance—it wasn't just having
fun and moving to music.

I knew that bees have long and elaborate dances
and by doing them they communicate lots of information about routes and distances, and how to get from
place to place. The dance I now joined was something
like that, but a thousand times more elaborate. As
we moved around the ballroom, sometimes gliding,

sometimes shuffling, sometimes jumping, and sometimes wiggling our bottoms, I could feel my brain being filled with knowledge.

I saw history. I experienced the story of the ancient space-faring pussycat race. Very ancient pussycats had discovered they could transform themselves into beings made entirely of light, traverse immense distances, and then reconstitute themselves into physical form. I learned the stories of the first journeys of exploration and the names of the great pussycat voyagers, heard the ancient songs, and saw great cities on unheard-of worlds.

I did not learn just big things. I learned the history of my own family. I saw my own parents, of whom I had never had any memory. The sight of them was incredibly sweet, and at the same time I felt hot tears squirting. Then I learned how they had left me temporarily with Uncle Father Palabra and then were lost on a journey, and so far not found—and I learned where it would make sense to begin looking for them. At this precise point, Molly passed me in the dance and whispered, "I'll go with you."

Then, for I don't know how long, the dance was about higher mathematics. Well, better to say *much* higher mathematics. I couldn't believe I was understanding the stuff that was being loaded into my head—but

I was. Then there was a lot of astro-navigation, and recipes, and poetry, and cookery. I was pretty sure not all of this would stay in my brain, at least anywhere in my brain where I could lay hands on it, when the dance was over.

And then . . . the dance was over. Dawn was breaking and the guests had said goodbye to one another, and all of them to Elizabeth and me, and had departed. I was standing on the veranda of Spookhuizen with Molly and Elizabeth.

"Well, that was certainly fun, wasn't it?" Elizabeth said.

"It's funny talking to two of you," Molly said. "I mean, talking to one of you, twice. So what are you, individually and collectively, going to do now?"

"I don't know," I said.

"I don't know," Elizabeth said.

"I have to think about it," I said.

"I have to think about it," Elizabeth said.

"I bet I know," Molly said.

"We bet you do," we both said.

(To be continued in *Escape to Dwerg Mountain,* soon to be available at the Gleybners' bookstore, in Poughkeepsie, New York.)